2023. 2 김선호

갯마을 차차차 포토 에세이 출간을 축하드립니다.

갯마을 차차차 포토에세이

2

갯마을 차차차

포토에세이 2

초판 1쇄 발행 2023년 2월 14일
초판 2쇄 발행 2023년 3월 14일

제작 | 스튜디오드래곤

펴낸이 | 金禎珉
펴낸곳 | 북로그컴퍼니
책임편집 | 김나정
디자인 | 김승은

사진 | [STILL ALIVE]한성경
포스터 사진 | 강현인
번역 | 정진서(Jinsuh Jung-Aum)

주소 | 서울시 마포구 와우산로 44(상수동), 3층
전화 | 02-738-0214
팩스 | 02-738-1030
등록 | 제2010-000174호

ISBN 979-11-6803-045-9　04810
　　　979-11-6803-043-5　04810 (세트)

우리의 마음이 춤추기 시작한 순간

포토에세이

2

갯마을 차차차

북로그컴퍼니

Contents

9 당신의 자리가, 일상을 그리는 순간
The moment your existence becomes a part of my daily life ⋯⋯ 6

10 당신의 사랑이, '우리'에 도달한 순간
The moment you and I became "us" ⋯⋯ 44

11 당신의 설렘이, 나의 행복이 되는 순간
The moment your excitement became my happiness ⋯⋯ 120

12 당신의 바람이, '함께'를 꿈꾸는 순간
The moment you dream of us "together" ⋯⋯ 186

13 당신의 오늘이, 내일을 바라는 순간 ······ 246
The moment you begin to look forward to our future together

14 당신의 약속이, 용기를 끌어낸 순간 ······ 282
The moment your promise gave me confidence

15 당신의 슬픔이, 봄을 맞이한 순간 ······ 318
The moment your sadness meets spring

16 우리의 인생이, 모두와 춤추는 순간 ······ 370
The moment everyone dances together

Behind story ······ 462

9

당신의 자리가, 일상을 그리는 순간
The moment your existence becomes a part of my daily life

간밤의 포옹으로 잠 못 이룬 혜진과 두식의 심장을 더 쿵쾅쿵쾅하게 할 하루가 기다리고 있었으니, 혜진의 아버지 태화와 새어머니 명신의 공진 방문! 하필이면 두 분, 혜진과 두식이 밤에 부둥켜안고 있었느니 하룻밤을 보냈다느니 하는 남숙의 말까지 들어버렸다. 누가 봐도 연인으로 오해할 수밖에 없는 상황에 두식은 혜진에게 오늘만 잘 넘겨보자며 일일 남자친구 대행 아르바이트를 제안한다.

두 사람이 역할극을 한다는 소식이 공진에 빠르게 퍼지고, 마을 사람들은 상품으로 걸린 윤치과 30% 할인권을 받기 위해 태화와 명신 앞에서 '선남선녀', '최고의 커플'이라며 혜진과 두식을 향한 칭찬을 아끼지 않는다. 네 사람은 우연히 성현을 만나 감리네 집 촬영 현장을 둘러보는 등 공진을 구경하며 하루를 보낸다. 두식과 종일 옆에 붙어 격 없는 대화를 나누고, 좋아하는 바둑까지 둔 태화. 반말이나 찍찍 하는 두식이지만 어쩐지 좀 마음에 든다. 혜진 또한 두식의 존재 하나로 부모님과 함께하는 시간이 참으로 따뜻하다. 하지만 두식이 가족 하나 없이 자랐단 말에 마음의 문을 닫아버리는 태화. 평생 외롭게 자란 혜진 걱정 때문이다. 그럼에도 "그 친구 옆에 정말 좋은 사람이 있길 바라요."라는 두식의 진심에 "그게… 자네일 수도 있잖아." 무심히 툭 진심을 뱉는 태화다.

연인 행세를 하는 두 사람을 보며 이번에는 결코 후회하지 않으리 결심한 성현. 태화의 말에 용기가 생긴 두식. 그렇게 그들은 각자의 자리에서 속도를 높여 혜진에게 향한다.

After hugging each other last night, Hye-jin and Du-sik have trouble falling asleep. Little do they know that they have a much more exciting day waiting ahead of them. In the town, rumors are rampant that Hye-jin and Du-sik were hugging each other very passionately last night. Hye-jin's father and stepmother, who have just come down to visit Gongjin, hear this rumor along with the word that Hye-jin and Du-sik have spent a night together. Hye-jin's father misunderstands that the two are dating. In order to "survive" the day with Hye-jin's somewhat conservative and scary father, Du-sik offers to work as Hye-jin's part-time boyfriend for the day.

The news that Hye-jin and Du-sik are pretending to be a couple spread quickly throughout Gongjin. To win a 30% discount coupon for the Yoon Dental Clinic, the townspeople eagerly contribute to the act, saying things like Hye-jin and Du-sik are the "best match" and "the town's number 1 couple." The four of them—Du-sik, Hye-jin, her father and stepmother—oincidentally meet Seong-hyeon. With him, they tour the filming site at Ms. Gam-ri's house and spend the day exploring Gongjin. Despite how Hye-jin's father initially disliked Du-sik for the way he talked down to him, after talking, playing Baduk, and spending the entire day with Du-sik, Hye-jin's reserved father begins to get fond of him. Hye-jin, much to her surprise, is able to enjoy her time with her father and stepmother because Du-sik is there. However, whatever progress Du-sik makes in gaining Hye-jin's father's favorability is lost when Hye-jin's father hears that Du-sik grew up without a family. This is because Hye-jin's father worries how this will affect Hye-jin, who also grew up very lonely. Du-sik says "I hope that Hye-jin will have a good man by her side." Hearing this, Hye-jin's father replies, "That man could be you." Du-sik feels encouraged by those words.

Seeing Hye-jin and Du-sik pretending to be a couple, Seong-hyeon decides that he shouldn't regret not telling his true feelings to Hye-jin this time. And thus, both Seong-hyeon and Du-sik gain more motivation to deepen their relationship with Hye-jin and head to her house.

저기 휴대폰...
여기다 놓고 갈게요.
하던 거 마저 하세요.

Excuse me, you dropped your phone...
I'll just leave it here.
Go back to whatever you two were doing.

핸드폰이 안 깨졌다.
역시 우리나라가 핸드폰을 잘 만들어.

그치! 우리나라가 IT 강국이니까.

My phone didn't crack.
Of course! Korea is good at making sturdy phones.

Right? Korea is an IT powerhouse after all.

조심히 들어가.

Get home safe!

결제 방법은 뭘로 하실 거야? 카드? 현금?
자, 카드 넣으셔, 카드.

How are you going to pay? With card or in cash?
Here, put your card in.

좀 전에 저 친구 나한테 반말한 거 맞지?

Just now, didn't that fellow speak down to me?

나 다 알아.
어젯밤에 막 홍반장이랑 꼭 끌어안고
블루스 추고 난리도 아니었다며?

I know everything.
I heard you and Chief Hong were passionately embracing each other last night.

걱정하지 마.
나 아무한테도 얘기 안 했으니까. 나만 믿어.

Don't worry.
I haven't told anyone. Trust me.

자네가 홍반장이란 말이지?
혜진이 아비일세.

대충 짐작은 했어.
기름은 잘 넣으셨지?

내 딸이랑 어떤 사이인가?
내 듣자 하니 둘이 하룻밤을 같이 보냈다던데? 아닌가?

아, 그게... 아닌 건 아닌데, 맞다고 하기에는 좀.

밤에 둘이 부둥켜안고 있었다던데?

네, 맞습니다.
저 치과, 아니 혜진이 남자친구입니다.

So you're Chief Hong?
I'm Hye-jin's father.

I had a rough idea.
Were you able to fill your car with gas all right?

What's your relationship with my daughter?
I heard you two spent the night together. Am I wrong?

Oh, that's... It's not that it's true, but to say that it's wrong is a little...

I also heard you two embraced each other last night.

Yes, that's right.
I'm Ms. Dentist's, no, Hye-jin's boyfriend.

대체 어쩌자고 그런 말을 한 거야?

오늘만 넘기려고.
오늘 하루 알바 쓴다고 생각해.
일일 남자친구 대행.

Why did you say something like that?

To survive today.
Just think of me as your part-timer.
Your boyfriend for the day.

혜진이 너 지금 백수를 만난다는 거냐?

제가 잘 버는데 남자 직업이 뭐가 중요해요?
사람만 괜찮으면 됐지!
그리고 홍반장 아빠가 생각하는 그런 무능력한 사람 아니에요.
이 얼굴에, 이 키에, 그리고 서울대까지 나왔다고요! 그것도 수석입학!
아빠 딸 그렇게 사람 보는 눈 없지 않아요.

Hye-jin, are you really dating someone who's unemployed?

What's so important about his job when I make good money?

It should be okay as long as he's a good guy!

And Chief Hong isn't as incompetent as you think.

Look at his face, his height, and he's even graduated from Seoul National University!

He got in with the highest grades, you know!

Dad, I have a good eye for people.

동네가 아담하니 좋네.

This neighborhood is nice and cozy.

윤선생님이랑 홍반장님이시다.
우리 동네 최고의 커플이 아니랄까 봐,
선남선녀가 따로 없다.

그러게.
나의 친구 두식이는 오늘도 참으로 멋지구나.

동네가 어째 좀 이상한 것 같은데?

If it isn't Dr. Yoon and Chief Hong.
No other couple in this neighborhood can compare
to this perfect pair.

True.
My friend Du-sik looks very handsome today, as always.

I'm starting to think this neighborhood is a little weird.

지금 언니네 부모님 오셔서 삼촌이 일일 남친 대행 중이래요. 대박이죠?

뭐? 말도 안 돼! 왜? 왜!

Hye-jin's parents are here so uncle is pretending to be her boyfriend! Isn't that crazy?

What? No way! Why?

안녕하십니까. 저는 혜진이 대학 선배 지성현이라고 합니다.
만나 뵙게 돼서 영광입니다, 아버님.

아버님? 허허... 듣기 좋으네.

Hello! I am Hye-jin's senior from college, Ji Seong-hyeon.
It's an honor to meet you father.

"Father"? Haha. I like the sound of that.

저희는 교양수업 때 처음 만났었어요.
발표까지 도맡아서 다들 찍소리도 못 하게 발표를 막, 다다닥, 말로 막.
아버님. 혜진이 말싸움 잘하는 거 아세요?

아, 완전 쌈닭이지.

We first met in an elective course.
She was in charge of the presentation for our group project and she did such an outstanding job.
Father, did you know that Hye-jin is good at debates?

Of course, she's a feisty one.

어르신들 잘 부탁해. 오늘 딱 하루 알바겠지만.

응, 오늘만큼은 내 역할에 충실할 예정이야.
치과 남자친구 대행.

I know you're just a one-day part-timer, but make sure to treat her parents well.

Of course, I'm really going to devote myself to my role
as Ms. Dentist's boyfriend today.

아버지, 가다가 졸리시면은 갓길에 차 세워.
안 그럼 큰일 나서!

자네 잠깐 이쪽으로 좀 와보게.

Father, if you get sleepy while driving, make sure to pull over.
If you don't it could be dangerous!

You, come over here for a second.

너 왜 자꾸 나한테 반말하냐?

아, 그게 내 철학인데. 친근하고 좋잖아.

너나 좋지, 이 새끼야.

Why do you keep talking down to me?

Oh, that's just a philosophy of mine. Isn't it more friendly and nice that way?

Maybe nice for you, you bastard.

아빠가 뭐라셔?

예? 예? 어...

What did dad say?

Pardon? Pardon? Uh...

10

당신의 사랑이, '우리'에 도달한 순간
The moment you and I became "us"

두식과 성현이 혜진에게 향하던 순간, 한발 앞서 혜진의 집에 찾아든 이가 있었으니. 공진을 흉흉하게 한 납치 미수범! 때마침 도착한 두식이 혜진을 구하고 범인을 붙잡는다.

졸지에 사건 현장이 되어버린 혜진의 집. 혜진은 두식의 집에서 하루를 보내기로 하는데 유독 바람이 요란하고 개들이 시끄럽게 짖어대는 밤이다. 혜진은 차마 혼자 잠들 수 없고 두식은 그런 혜진을 위해 시 한 편을 읽어준다. 그렇게 혜진은 소파에서 잠들고, 담요 하나를 나눠 덮은 두식도 바닥에서 잠이 든다.

다음 날은 두식 할아버지의 제삿날. 두식이 외로울까 걱정이 된 혜진은 제사상에 올릴 전을 사서 두식을 찾는데, 혜진의 걱정이 무색하게 하나둘 모여들어 손을 보태는 마을 사람들. 두식을 향한 공진 사람들의 따뜻한 마음에 혜진은 다행스럽다. 혜진과 두식은 다들 떠나고 둘만 남은 집에서 제사를 지내고, 음식을 나눠 먹으며 둘만 아는 설렘의 시간을 또 한 번 쌓는다.

한편, 더는 늦어지면 안 될 것 같아 혜진에게 고백하는 성현이고, 마음이 복잡해진 혜진은 미선과 서울 나들이에 나서는데 무얼 해도 두식이 생각나 혼란스럽다. 비까지 내리자 빗속에서 함께 뛰놀던 추억에 더이상 참을 수 없는 혜진! 공진으로 달려가 두식에게 사랑을 고백한다. 이에 두식은 키스로 답하고, 둘은 비로소 서로의 마음을 확인한다.

Before either Du-sik and Seong-hyeon can arrive at Hye-jin's house, someone else gets there first. It is the criminal who has been stirring up trouble in Gongjin! Du-sik arrives just in time to save Hye-jin and catch the criminal.

Suddenly, Hye-jin's house becomes a crime scene. Hye-jin decides to spend the night at Du-sik's place. Still paranoid from the incident, the loud sounds of wind and dogs barking keep Hye-jin up. Hye-jin cannot fall asleep alone, so Du-sik reads her poems. Soon, the two fall asleep sharing the same blanket: Hye-jin on the couch and Du-sik on the floor. The next day is the memorial service day for Du-sik's grandfather. Worried that Du-sik might be feeling lonely, Hye-jin buys jeon for him. She soon realizes that her worries were for nothing after seeing how all of the townspeople have brought food and gathered at Du-sik's place. Hye-jin feels thankful for the warm hearts of the people in Gongjin. After everyone leaves, Hye-jin and Du-sik hold the memorial service, eat the leftover food, and spend quality time together.

Seong-hyeon feels that he shouldn't wait any longer and confesses to Hye-jin. Hye-jin, whose mind has suddenly become very complicated after the confession, heads to Seoul with Mi-seon. No matter what she does, Hye-jin keeps thinking of Du-sik. It starts raining and Hye-jin recalls when she and Du-sik played in the rain. Hye-jin realizes her feelings and rushes to Gongjin. She confesses her love to Du-sik. He replies with a kiss, and the two finally confirm their feelings for each other.

누, 누, 누구세요?
누군데 남의 집에 함부로 들어와?

신고하려고? 이제 너 도와줄 사람 아무도 없다.

Wh-Wh-Who are you?

Who are you to enter my house?

Are you trying to call the police? There's no one to help you now.

나쁜 놈 잡기 좋은 밤이다. 그렇지?

What a good night to catch a bad guy, right?

어디 다친 데 없어?
어디 다친 데 없는 거지, 진짜?

Are you hurt anywhere?
You're really okay, right?

혜진아!!!

Hye-jin!!!

다행히 신경 손상은 없어서
바로 봉합하시면 되겠네요.

다행이다. 아프진 않아?

Fortunately there was no nerve damage,
so a few stitches will be enough.

That's a relief. Does it hurt?

그 멍은 뭐야? 다쳤어?

아... 아무것도 아니야.

아무것도 아니긴! 다쳤잖아!
얼마나 다친 거야? 아프진 않아?

...홍반장이 훨씬 다쳤거든?

치과... 울어?

진짜, 놀라가지고.
아니, 그렇게 칼 들고 덤비는데 뛰어드는 사람이 어디 있어!

나는 너 다칠까 봐 그랬지.

What's that bruise? Are you hurt?

Oh... This is nothing.

What do you mean nothing? You're hurt!
How bad did you get hurt? Does it hurt?

...Chief Hong, your injury is way worse.

Ms. Dentist... are you crying?

God, I was so scared.
What kind of person jumps at a guy holding a knife?

I was just worried he might hurt you.

홍반장,
혜진이 구해줘서 고마워, 진짜로.

Chief Hong,
Thank you for saving Hye-jin.
Really, I mean it.

이제 어떡할래?

뭘?

So, what do you want to do now?

About what?

오늘 밤 말이야. 집이 졸지에 사건현장이 돼버렸잖아.

I mean tonight. Since your place became a crime scene.

옷이 좀 큰 것 같아.

I think the clothes are too big for me.

크기는! 아주 맞춤옷처럼 딱 맞는구만.
치과가 어우, 어깨가 좋아.

They're not too big! They fit you perfectly.
Ms. Dentist, you have such nice broad shoulders.

할아버지 생각 많이 나?

Do you think of your grandfather a lot?

...아니. 생각이 잘 안 나.
하나도 안 까먹고 기억하고 싶은데 자꾸 희미해져.
할아버지 목소리, 눈빛, 손...

... No. I don't remember him well.
I want to remember everything about him, but my memories keep fading.
His voice, his gaze, and his hands...

심장마비였어. 너무 늦게 발견했고.
내가 월드컵 응원한다고 밖에 놀러 가지만 않았어도...

그랬으면 할아버지가 안 돌아가셨을 거라고,
설마 그렇게 생각해온 거야?
지금까지 그런 바보 같은 생각을 해왔다니.
아주 할아버지가 하늘에서 복장 터지셨겠다!
근데 홍반장, 자기 얘기한 거 처음이네.

그러게.
내가 이런 얘기한 사람...
살면서 네가 두 번째다.

He had a heart attack, but he was found too late.
If only I hadn't gone out to cheer for the World Cup...

Don't tell me you think if you didn't go out,
he wouldn't have passed away.
I can't believe you've been thinking such a stupid thing for
this long.
Your grandfather in heaven must be so frustrated!
You know, Chief Hong, this is the first time you talked about
yourself.

I guess you're right.
You're the second person...
I've told these stories to.

설마 또 누가 들어오는 건 아니겠지?

원하면 내일 당장 대문 달아줄게.
아니다, 그냥 지뢰를 깔자. 그니까 안심하라고.

There's no way someone might break in again, right?

If you want, I'll fix your front gate tomorrow.
Scratch that, let's plant mines instead. I'm just saying you should relax.

읽는다.
그냥 들어도 좋고,
잠 오면 더 좋고.

I'll start reading now.
You can just listen,
or, even better, just fall asleep.

홍반장... 할아버지 얘기... 처음 해준 사람... 누구야.

있어. 어떤 사람.
아주 따뜻했던 사람.

에이씨.

Chief Hong... who was the first person you told the story
about your grandfather to?

It was someone
who was very warm hearted.

Damn it.

어젯밤에는 어쩌다가 홍반장이 구해주게 된 거야?
그러니까 설마 그 야심한 밤에 둘이 같이 있었나?
지금도 이렇게 둘이 짠 하고 나타나가지고.

How did Chief Hong end up saving you last night?
Were you two together that late at night?
Even now the two of you showed up together.

근데 왜 자꾸 따라와?
이러다 치과까지 같이 출근하겠어.

응. 그러려고.

Why do you keep following me?
At this rate you're going to end up at the clinic with me.

Yup, that was the plan.

우리 할아버지 잡수라고 사온 거 아니야?
이거 시장 전집에서 샀지?
우리 할아버지가 여기 깻잎전을 엄청 좋아했어.
치과 셀렉이 기가 막히네.

나는 이만 가볼게.
할아버지랑 오붓한 시간 보내.

있고 싶으면 있어도 돼.

어?

...있고 싶으면.

Didn't you buy this for my grandpa?

It's from the market, right?

My grandpa really loved the perilla leaf jeon from here.

You have a great taste for good food.

I'll be on my way now.

Have a nice time with your grandfather.

You can stay if you want.

What?

...only if you want to.

뭐야? 이거 나 먹으라고 준 거야?

멀쩡할 때도 안 먹던 걸 그 팔로 잘도 까먹겠다.

잘 먹을게.

새우도 그렇고 게도 그렇고 갑각류 너무 귀찮아.
들인 공에 비하면 진짜 알맹이는 요만해.
근데 또 맛은 있어.

그러게.
생각해보니까 이 귀찮은 걸 해주는 사람이 할아버지밖에 없었네.

그래! 껍질 까주는 게 진짜 보통 일이 아니야.
웬만큼의 애정이 있지 않고서는 진짜 못할 짓이라니까?
어... 그게... 지금은 불가항력에 의한 특수 상황.
홍반장 다쳤잖아, 나 때문에.

어. 맞아. 나 전치 4주다. 아, 아파.

What are you doing? Did you just peel this for me?

It must be hard to eat with your injured arm.

Thanks for the food.

Shrimps and crabs are so much work to eat.
Compared to the effort you put in, the yield is too small.
But they're delicious.

That's true.
Come to think of it, my grandpa was the only one who would do this bothersome thing for me.

Yeah, peeling these is no ordinary task.
It takes a lot of love to do this much for someone else.
Oh... well... this is an exception.
You got injured because of me.

Oh, you're right. It's going to take 4 weeks for me to recover. Ow, it hurts.

혜진아. 내가 살면서 후회하는 게 딱 하나가 있는데...
너한테 고백 못 한 거. 14년 전에 너한테 고백 못 한 거 두고두고 후회했어.
근데 여기 공진에서 너를 다시 만나게 됐고, 되게 오래 고민했어.
내 감정이 과거의 애틋했던 마음인지 아니면은 현재의 떨림인지.

Hye-jin, there's only one thing I regret in life...
It's the fact that I never told you how I felt. I regret not being able to confess to you 14 years ago.
But I met you again here in Gongjin, and I've been thinking about it for a long time.
I wasn't sure at first whether these feelings were due to my past feelings for you
or if they're my current feelings towards you.

그러고서 내가 내린 결론은... 내가 너를 좋아해.
부담 가질 필요도 없고, 당장 대답해달라는 것도 아니야.
그냥 더 늦기 전에 말하고 싶었어, 너한테.
이번에는 후회하기 싫었거든.

And the conclusion I ended up with is that... I like you.
You don't have to feel pressured, and I don't need an immediate answer.
I just wanted to tell you before it was too late.
I don't want to have any regrets this time.

할아바이. 오늘 친구 와서 좀 시끄러웠지?
걔가 원래 좀 그래. 따발따발 말도 좀 많고 웃기도 잘 웃고.

Gramps. My friend was a little loud today, right?
That's just how she is. She's very talkative and full of laughter.

그래도 있다가 없으니까 좀 허전하네.

Still, it feels a little empty here now that she's gone.

그럼 그때 그 꼬맹이가 치과였어?

Then that little girl from back then was Ms. Dentist?

두식이 니 치과선생한테 마음이 있지?
그득하니 마음이 만선인데, 어데서 계속 그짓불이나!
두식아... 인생 지다한 것 같아도 살아보믄 짧아.
쓸데없는 생각 쳐내꼰져버리고, 니 스스로한테 솔직하라니.

Du-sik, ya have feelings for the dentist, right?

It's obvious she's taken up all the space in yer heart. Why do you keep lying to ya'self?

Du-sik... life may seem long, but when ya live it, it's actually very short.

Don't think unnecessary thoughts and just be honest to ya'self.

홍반장!
홍반장 안에 없어?

Chief Hong!
Chief Hong, are you home?

좋아해! 나 홍반장 좋아해!
나는 99살까지 인생시간표를 짜놓은 계획형 인간이야.
선 넘는 거 싫어하는 개인주의자에, 비싼 신발을 좋아해.
홍반장이랑은 정반대지.
혈액형 궁합도 MBTI도 어느 하나 잘 맞는 게 하나도 없을걸.
크릴새우 먹는 펭귄이랑 바다사자 잡아먹는 북극곰만큼 다를 거야.
근데 그런 거 다 모르겠고, 내가 홍반장을 좋아해.

치과, 나는...

아무 말도 하지 마!
그냥 뭐 어떻게 해달라고 하는 거 아니야.
어, 자꾸 내 마음이 부풀어 올라서
이러다가 아무 때나 빵 터져버릴 것 같아.
나도 어쩔 수가 없어.

I like you! I like you Chief Hong!
I'm someone who tries to plan for every second until I'm 99 years old.
I don't like people crossing the line, I'm very independent, and I like expensive
shoes.
In other words, I'm the complete opposite of you.
Even our blood types and MBTIs are incompatible.
We're probably as different as penguins that eat krill and polar bears that eat
sea lions.
But even so, I like Chief Hong.

Ms. Dentist, I...

Don't say anything!
I'm not asking you to do anything.
It's just that my feelings keep getting bigger
and it feels like it could overflow at any second.
I can't help it.

...나도.
나도 이제 더는
어쩔 수가 없다.

...Me too.
I can't help it either.

11

당신의 설렘이, 나의 행복이 되는 순간
The moment your excitement became my happiness

드디어 서로의 마음을 확인한 혜진과 두식. 하지만 혜진은 두식과 사귀기 전 성현에게 예의를 갖추고 싶다 말하고, 성현과 혜진은 애틋했던 인연에 종지부를 찍는다.

한편, 혜진은 동네에 별별 소문이 떠도는 게 싫어 두식에게 비밀 연애를 제안하고, 두식은 공진 바닥에서 과연 몰래 사귀는 게 가능할까 싶지만 혜진의 의견에 따르기로 한다. 하지만 혜진과 두식은 보고 싶은 마음을 참을 수 없는 이제 막 연애를 시작한 커플이고, 어디에서 꽁냥거리든 계속해서 마을 사람들에게 발각될 위기에 처한다. 상황을 모면하기 위해 그때마다 싸우는 척 두식을 밀어내는 혜진! 라이브카페에서는 뺨을 맞고 윤치과에서는 정강이를 까이고 보라슈퍼에서는 머리를 맞는 두식이다.

하지만 역시나 비밀이란 없는 공진! 둘의 연애를 일찌감치 눈치챈 마을 사람들은 둘을 일부러 갈라놓기로 작전을 짠다. 참다못한 혜진과 두식이 연애 사실을 먼저 실토하도록 하는 게 이 작전의 목표! 마을 사람들의 작전에 더해 휴대폰까지 잃어버린 두식! 연락을 할 수도, 만날 수도 없어 애가 타던 두 사람이 드디어 서로를 향해 돌진하는 순간, 모두 모인 마을 사람들에게 현장을 발각당하고 만다. 더 이상 그 무엇도 참을 수 없는 혜진과 두식은 사람들 앞에서 당당히 연애 사실을 선언한다.

Despite having confirmed their mutual feelings, Hye-jin puts their relationship on hold so she can reply to Seong-hyeon's confession.

Hye-jin doesn't like the idea of more rumors circulating in the town, so she suggests to Du-sik that they keep their relationship a secret. Even though Du-sik wonders if a secret relationship is even possible in this nosy town, he decides to follow Hye-jin's desire. But as a new couple that has just started dating, it is hard to hide their lovey-dovey relationship. Each time someone comes close, Hye-jin pretends to be fighting with Du-sik; she slaps him at the live music cafe, kicks him at her clinic, and hits his head at the Bora Supermarket.

But, as expected, there's no hiding secrets in Gongjin. The townspeople notice the two's relationship early on, and deliberately plan to keep them apart. The goal of this strategy is to get Hye-jin and Du-sik to confess that they're in a relationship. Meanwhile, as the townspeople are carrying out this plan, Du-sik loses his phone. Unable to meet and, now, unable to contact each other, Du-sik and Hye-jin start to miss each other. When they try to secretly meet, the two are once again discovered. Finally at their limit, Hye-jin and Du-sik proudly declare their relationship in front of the townspeople.

좋아해.
그렇게 저돌적인 고백을 받아놓고,
그냥 퉁치고 넘어가면 비겁하지.
나도 치과 좋아해. 그렇게 됐어.
아니, 그렇게 돼버렸어.

우리 키스도 했고 서로 좋아하고...
그럼 어떻게 되는 거야?

뭘 어떻게, 이렇게 되는 거지. 가자.

I like you.
You gave me such a sincere confession,
it would be cowardly of me to not give you a proper reply.
I like you too. It just turned out like that.
No, I couldn't help it.

So now that we kissed and that our feelings are mutual...
what's next?

What do you think? It's this. Let's go!

우리 사귀는 거 며칠만 보류하자.
성현 선배가 고백을 했어.

Let's put off officially dating for a few days.

It's just that Seong-hyeon sunbae confessed to me.

홍반장 질투해?

고백을 받은 사람이 대처해야 될 자세에 대해서 하는 얘기야.
상대가 서브를 날렸으면 그걸 받아쳐야지. 그걸 왜 피해?
인인지 아웃인지 정확하게 얘기를 지금 해줘야 될 거 아니야!

그러는 홍반장은?
선배 마음 알고 있었으면서 왜 가만히 있었어?
다른 사람이 나 좋아해도 별로 상관없었던 건 아니고?

그야... 그때는 내가 너 그만큼 좋아하는지 몰랐으니까!

그만큼이 얼마만큼인데?

양으로나 질적으로나 너 섭섭지 않을 만큼은 될걸?
그냥 뭐 바이칼 호 정도는 돼!

Chief Hong, are you jealous?

I'm just teaching you about good manners for when someone confesses to you.
If someone serves the ball to you, you have to hit it back. You can't dodge!
You have to give a clear answer whether the ball is in or out!

Then what about you?
Why didn't you do anything if you knew about sunbae's feelings?
Is it because you don't care if someone else likes me?

That's because I didn't know how much I liked you back then!

So exactly how much do you like me?

In terms of both quantity and quality,
I'm sure it's enough that you wouldn't be disappointed.
It's as big as Lake Baikal.

저도 사실 선배 좋아했어요.
근데 선배 마음, 내 마음 알면서도 모른 척했어요.
자신이 없었거든요. 선배한테 내 가장 초라한 모습을 들켜버린 것 같아서.
그때 솔직하지 못했던 거 제가 얼마나 후회하며 살았는지 몰라요.
그래서 지금이라도 선배한테 솔직하고 싶어요.
미안해요, 선배. 나 좋아하는 사람이 있어요.

To be honest, I actually liked you too.

Even though I knew you liked me too, I chose to ignore it.

Because I wasn't confident that'd it work out. After all, you had seen me at my lowest.

I've always regretted not being honest to myself back then.

So I want to be honest to you this time around.

I'm sorry sunbae. There's someone else I like.

다행이다.
예전의 윤혜진처럼 그리고 나처럼 머뭇거리지 않고
이렇게 용감하게 얘기할 수 있게 돼서 다행이다.
근데 혜진아. 너 하나도 안 초라했어.
나는 단 한 순간도 열심히 살지 않은 적이 없는 너를,
그리고 항상 자기 자신을 지킬 줄 아는 너를, 있는 그대로 좋아했어.
그런 네가 내 첫사랑이라서 참 영광이야, 혜진아.

I'm relieved.

You didn't hesitate the way we did in the past.

I'm so relieved that you were able to bravely tell me your honest feelings.

But you know, Hye-jin. That, back then, wasn't your lowest.

I really admired how you worked your hardest everyday,

and how you never lost your pride, no matter what. I loved you for the way you were.

I'm truly honored that someone like you was my first love.

혜진이한테 잘해줘.

많이 웃게 해주고, 밥은 꼭 맛있는 걸로 먹이고.

내가 단순한 사람이라서 그런가 복잡한 게 싫더라.

인간관계에 더하기 빼기 곱하기 나누기... 아유, 막 머리 아파.

Treat Hye-jin well.

Make her laugh a lot, and make sure to always treat her to good food.

Maybe it's because I'm a simple person, but I really don't like complicated things.

I don't like calculating human relationships... it gives me a headache.

나 혜진이 좋아해.
근데, 내가 생각보다 홍반장도 좋아하는 것 같아.

I like Hye-jin.
But I realized that I'm more fond of Chief Hong than I thought.

나 오늘은 카페모카 줘. 휘핑크림 잔뜩.

왜? 아침부터 당 떨어져?

아니. 나 너무 달달해서 혈당 폭발.

Give me a café mocha today. With extra whipped cream.

Why? Are you running low on sugar this early in the morning?

No, my blood sugar's overflowing with sweetness.

홍반장! 말이 너무 심한 거 아니야? 짜증 나, 진짜.

너 뭐라 그런 거야?
뭐라 그랬길래 뺨따귀를 이렇게...

Chief Hong! Don't you think your words were too harsh? Ugh, I'm so annoyed.

What happened?
What'd you say for her to slap you in the face like this?

아까는 너무 미안했어. 당황해가지고.
아팠지? 내가 호 해줄게.

I'm so sorry about this morning. I just panicked.
It hurt, right? Let me blow on it for you.

윤선생, 생각보다 사람이 굉장히 폭력적이시네요.

Dr. Yoon, you're more violent than I thought.

아니, 어떻게 이 얼굴을 까먹을 수가 있지? 이렇게 똑같이 생겼는데.
귀여워... 진짜 귀여워 죽겠네.

How did I forget this face? He looks exactly the same.
So cute... He's too adorable.

화장실은 저기. 아시지?
잠깐 여기 앉아 계셔들.
방은 지저분하니까 들어가지 마시고.

The bathroom is over there. You know where it is, right?
Sit here for a second.
My room's messy so don't go in there.

홍반장, 아무리 바빠도 톡은 확인해.
나 연락 안 되는 거 싫어.

그럴게. 또 싫어하는 거 있어?
치과가 싫어하는 거 다 얘기해봐.

거짓말하는 거.
우리 둘 사이에는 비밀 같은 거 없었으면 좋겠어.

Chief Hong, no matter how busy you are, you should check your texts.
I don't like it when I can't contact you.

Okay, I will. Is there anything else you don't like?
Tell me everything you don't like.

I don't want you to lie.
I don't want there to be any secrets between the two of us.

어허! 에헤!
어디 지금 말을 섞으려고 그러세요.
둘은 앞으로 대화를 나누지 마.
둘은 맨날 싸우잖아. 거리를 둬.

Hey! Stop!

Don't try to talk to him.

You two shouldn't speak to each other from now on.

You always fight when you do, so keep your distance from each other.

형. 나 핸드폰이 없어졌어.

그거 찾을 때까지 당분간 연락이 좀 잘 안 될 것 같아.

나 연락 너무 안 돼도 걱정하지 말라고.

Hyung. I lost my phone.

I don't think you'll be able to contact me until I find it.

Don't worry too much even if you can't reach me.

만난 지 얼마나 됐다고 생이별이야.
홍반장은 왜 핸드폰을 잃어버려가지고 톡도 안 되고.
홍반장 목소리 듣고 싶다.

I can't believe we have to be apart when we just started dating.
Why did he have to lose his phone? I can't even text him now.
I want to hear Chief Hong's voice.

조사장님이... 직접 오셨네요?

당분간 홍반장은 여기 윤치과 배달 금지.
우리가 또 한다면 하는 사람들이거든, 응.

I didn't know you'd come yourself, Ms. Cho.

For the time being, Chief Hong won't be delivering food here.
We're keeping our word to keep you two separate.

너무 보고 싶었어!
나 이렇게 못 만나는 거 너무 싫어.
맨날맨날 보고 싶어.
맨날맨날 목소리 듣고 싶고 맨날맨날 껴안고 싶어.

I missed you so much!
I hate that we're not able to see each other.
I want to see you everyday.
I want to hear your voice everyday and I want to hug you everyday.

너 없이 34년을 살았는데,
널 알고 난 이 하루가 평생처럼 길다.
윤혜진, 너 뭐야? 너 나한테 무슨 짓을 한 거야?

한 번 더 불러줘.
내 이름...

혜진아. 윤혜진.

수천수만 번을 들었는데도 너무 낯설어. 꼭 새 이름 같아.

I lived without you for 34 years of my life,
but today felt like forever because I wasn't able to see you.
Yoon Hye-jin, who are you? What have you done to me?

Say it again.
My name...

Hye-jin. Yoon Hye-jin.

I've heard people say my name thousands of times,
but it sounds so unfamiliar now. It feels like a new name.

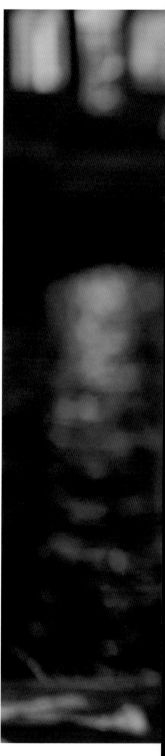

저희 사귀어요!
나 더 이상 숨기고 싶지 않아. 비밀 같은 거 안 키울래.
나 홍반장이랑 실컷 연애하고 싶어!
저희 사귀기로 했어요!

We're dating!
I don't want to hide it anymore or keep any secrets.
I want to date Chief Hong openly!
We decided to go out!

어, 알어.	Yeah, we know.
한 나흘 됐지?	What, has it been four days?
아니, 사흘.	No, three days.
잘됐싸. 차암 잘됐다니. 내거 인제 아무 여한이 없싸	I'm glad. I'm really happy for ya. Now I have nothing more to wish for.

다들 땡큐 베리 머치!
그럼 이 열화와 같은 성원에 힘입어 우리 열심히 잘 만나볼게!

Everyone, thank you very much!
Now that we have your enthusiastic support, we'll date openly!

12

당신의 바람이, '함께'를 꿈꾸는 순간
The moment you dream of us "together"

공개 연애를 시작한 혜진과 두식! 혜진은 데이트 버킷리스트를 작성하고, 두식은 그런 혜진이 귀엽기만 하다. 혜진의 소원을 들어주기 위해 두 사람은 서울 데이트를 감행한다. 혜진은 백화점에 들러 자신의 버킷리스트라며 두식의 정장을 사주고, 갖고 싶던 목걸이라며 주얼리 매장에서 무려 500만 원을 결제한다. 한편, 백화점에서 아는 사람을 만난 두식은 표정이 좋지 않고, 누군지 묻는 혜진에게는 '대학 선배'라고 짧게 답할 뿐 자세한 이야기를 하지 않는다.

공진으로 돌아온 두 사람. 어쩐지 기류가 좋지 않다. 혜진은 자신이 너무 돈 자랑을 한 것 같아 가뜩이나 마음 쓰이는데 두식은 문자에도 전화에도 반응이 시큰둥하다. 답답함에 두식의 집을 찾은 혜진. 한참이 지나서야 집으로 돌아온 두식은 밖에서 이야기하자며 혜진을 인적 드문 바닷가로 데리고 가는데, 이 세상에 단둘만 존재하는 것 같은 너무나 아름다운 바다다. 타프와 꼬마 전구와 피크닉 매트와 모닥불. 두식의 정성이 가득한 로맨틱한 바닷가. 그곳에서 혜진은 자신의 마음을 솔직히 털어놓고, 두식은 '네가 하는 모든 행동들에 날 신경 쓸 필요는 없다'며 혜진을 따스히 감싼다. 그렇게 서로의 가장 깊은 진심을 나눈 두 사람. 하늘에는 별이 가득하고 파도가 두 사람을 향해 노래하는 아름다운 밤이다.

Hye-jin and Du-sik start publicly dating! Hye-jin writes a bucket list of things to do with her boyfriend, and Du-sik finds this very cute. To grant one of Hye-jin's bucket list wishes, the two go on a date in Seoul. Hye-jin stops by the department store to buy Du-sik clothes, saying that it's on her bucket list. She buys an expensive necklace that's over 5 million won (approx. $4,000 USD) that she wanted for a long time. After Du-sik suddenly runs into someone he knows, his expression darkens. When Hye-jin asks who that was, Du-sik gives a vague reply that he's an upperclassman from college and does not go into further details.

The couple return to Gongjin. For some reason, Du-sik is in a bad mood. Hye-jin worries that she hurt Du-sik's feelings by showing off her money. She becomes more concerned when Du-sik only gives short replies to her calls and texts. In frustration, Hye-jin ends up visiting Du-sik's house. Du-sik returns home very late and takes Hye-jin to a beautiful, empty beach. Here, it feels as if they are the only two people to exist in the world. Du-sik had set up a romantic picnic with a tarp, picnic mat, bonfire, and strings of lights. Hye-jin shares her honest concerns with Du-sik, to which he replies "Hye-jin, you don't have to worry about how I'll view everything you do" and gives her a warm hug. The two shared their deepest feelings with each other. It's a beautiful night. The sky is full of stars and even the waves seem to be singing to the couple.

나 너무 행복해.

나도 행복해.

I'm so happy.

Me too.

★ Hye-jin's bucket list ★

Do couples yoga

개같이 생겨가지고.
큰 개. 얼굴 하얘가지고 쌍꺼풀 요렇게 있어가지고,
시고르자브종.

너는 고양이인데, 약간 개도 보여. 섞였어.

그럼 난 개냥이인가? 멍멍멍, 야옹야옹.

보조개 뽁뽁거리는 거 봐.

나만 있냐? 너도 있거든?

네가 더 깊거든?

네가 더 귀엽고 깊거든?

You look like a dog.

A big dog. With your pale skin and your deep double eyelids,

you look like a countryside mutt.

Well, you look like a cat with some dog features. You're a bit of both.

Then am I a "cat-dog"? Woof woof, meow.

Look at your cute dimple.

Am I the only one who has one? You have dimples too.

Yours are deeper.

Yours are cuter and deeper.

커플 궁합 보기

Take a couple's compatibility test

매운 음식 먹기

Eat spicy food

교복 입기

Wear school uniforms

함께 일출 보기.
커플 요가하기.
남자친구 면도해주기.
인생 맛집 데려가기.
이게 다 나랑 하고 싶은 거였어?
하자. 이렇게 귀여운데 어떻게 다 안 들어주고 배겨.

그러면 다음 주말에 서울 데이뚜 갈까?
각오해. 여기 있는 거 진짜 많이 지울 거야.

천천히 지워.
서두르지 말고,
여기 있는 거 하나하나씩 오래오래
그렇게 다 하자.

Watch the sunrise together.
Do couples yoga.
Give my boyfriend a shave.
Go to good restaurants together.
Is this everything you want to do with me?
Let's do all of them. How could I not, when you're this cute?

Can we go on a date in Seoul next weekend?
Prepare yourself, we'll be checking off a lot on this list.

Take it slowly.
You don't need to rush.
Let's do everything on this list together for a long time.

진짜 부럽다! 나도 동정이나 걱정받는 거 말고, 질투나 해봤으면 좋겠네.
어디 내 앞에서 딴 남자 얘기 하냐고 아주 큰소리 뻥뻥 치면서
아주 지랄발광이나 해봤으면 좋겠네, 아주 그냥.
이제 알겠냐? 그 사랑싸움이 얼마나 배부른 건지?

You're so lucky! I wish I could be jealous, instead of being pitied like this.

I wish I could get angry at her for talking about another guy in front of me. Damn it.

Do you get it know? Do you see how lucky you are to have these kind of love quarrels?

내가 미안해.

네 마음 알면서도 괜히 꼬투리 잡은 거.

엄한 사람 질투해서 혼자 삐지고 혼자 발작하고.

문도 그냥 막 닫고 나가버리고.

그리고 이제서야 사과하는 거.

난 진짜 내가 쿨한 줄 알았거든?

근데 생각보다 유치하고 구질구질하더라.

나 지피디 닭다리 뺏어 먹었다?

내가 윤혜진 때문에 매일 낯선 나를 발견하는 중이다, 정말.

나도 홍반장의 매력을 매일매일 발견하는 중이야.

오늘의 발견은... 귀여워.

I'm sorry.

I nagged at you even though I knew what you really meant.

I was sulking and acting jealous on my own,

and I slammed the door on my way out.

And I took so long to apologize.

I really thought I was a cool guy who wouldn't be affected by these kind of things.

But I'm more childish and pathetic than I thought.

I even stole his chicken drumsticks.

I'm discovering a new side to myself every day because of you.

I'm also discovering new charming sides to Chief Hong every day.

Today's discovery is that you're really cute.

나 오늘 고삐 풀렸어.
나 적토마야.
말리지 마!

Today, I'm uncontrollable.
My wallet is wide open!
Don't try to stop me!

남자친구 옷 사주는 것도 내 버킷리스트 포함이야.
그리고 조만간 홍반장 생일이잖아. 미리 해피 벌스데이 투 유야.

Buying my boyfriend's clothes is on my bucket list.
Besides, it's going to be your birthday soon. Happy early birthday to you.

난 이 세상의 모든 예쁜 것들이 좋아.

I like all the pretty things in this world.

너 이 자식 대체 이게 얼마 만이야. 너 인마 내가 얼마나 걱정했는 줄 알아?
죽었는지 살았는지 갑자기 연락도 안 되고.

How long has it been? Man, do you know how worried I was?
I suddenly lost contact with you, and I didn't even know if you were dead or alive.

내가 너무 돈 자랑하는 것처럼 느껴졌나?
괜히 목걸이 때문에 내가 너무 부담스러워진 건가?

Did it seem too much like I was bragging about my money?

Did he feel troubled because of the necklace?

홍반장, 우리 이따가 같이 저녁 먹을래?

어쩌지? 나 일이 늦게 끝날 것 같은데.
다음에 먹자.

Chief Hong, do you want to grab dinner with me later?

Sorry, I think I'll finish work late today.
Let's eat together next time.

나 할 얘기 있는데.

오늘은 밖에서 해.

I have something to say.

Let's talk outside today.

혜진아. 네가 하는 모든 행동들에 나 신경 쓸 필요 없어.
네가 열심히 일해서 번 돈으로 너한테 선물하는 건데, 왜 내 눈치를 봐?
나 아무렇지도 않아. 그러니까 너 하고 싶은 대로 하면 돼.

Hye-jin, you don't have to worry about how I'll view everything you do.
You bought yourself a gift with your own hard-earned money,
so why worry about what I think?
I don't mind, so do whatever you want.

그 목걸이 내가 사주고 싶었는데 너무 비싸더라.
그래서 그거 대신 담을 수 있는 보석함을 만든 건데...
이제 목걸이가 없네.

아니야! 나 다른 목걸이도 많고 귀걸이도 많고
이거 금방 채울 수 있어. 고마워 홍반장, 너무 예쁘다.

I wanted to buy that necklace for you, but it was too expensive.

So I made a jewelry box for it instead...

but you don't have the necklace anymore.

It's fine! I have a lot of other necklaces and earrings.

I can easily fill this box up. Thank you Chief Hong, it's so pretty.

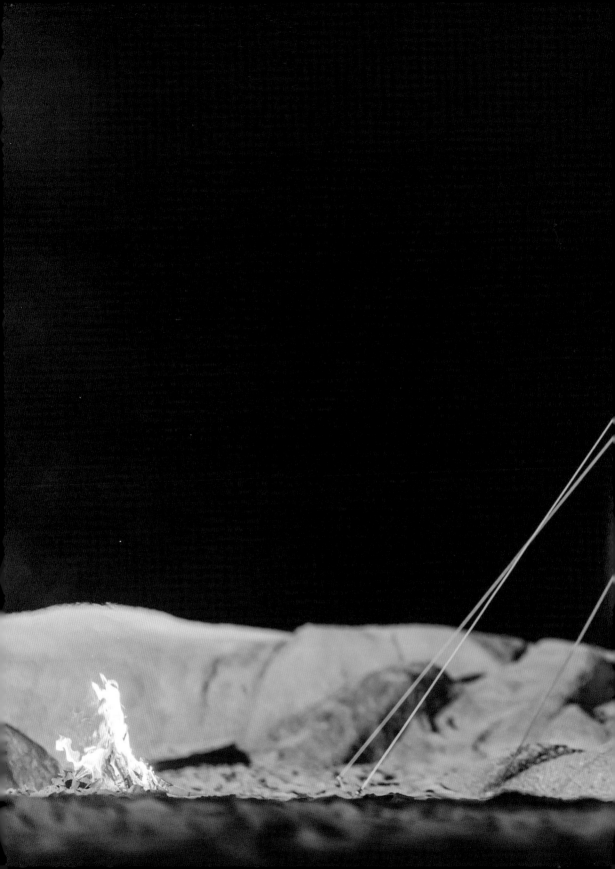

내가 제일 좋아하는 바다야.
바다가 다 똑같은 바다지,
뭐 이렇게 생각할 수 있겠지만.

아니야, 달라.
의미가 생기는 순간, 특별한 곳이 되니까.
여기 홍반장이 데려온 바다. 그래서 내가 좋아하게 된 바다.
나 지금 여기에 있는 모든 것이 너무 좋아.
모닥불, 파도 소리, 바닷소리, 여름 냄새, 별 그리고 너.
나 이 세상 어떤 것보다 네가 너무 좋아.

그러니까 이 말은 내가 먼저 해야겠다.
윤혜진, 사랑해.

나도 홍두식 사랑해.

It's my favorite place.
I know you might think
the ocean looks the same from everywhere.

No, it's different.
The moment a meaningful memory is made there, it becomes a special place.
Because this is the beach you took me to,
it's become one of my favorite places too.
I really love everything here.
The bonfire, the sound of the waves, the smell of summer, the stars, and you.
I like you more than anything in the world.

Alright then I should be the first one to say this,
Yoon Hye-jin, I love you.

Me too. I love you Hong Du-sik.

★ Du-sik's bucket list ★

Give her a handmade gift

13

당신의 오늘이, 내일을 바라는 순간
The moment you begin to look forward to our future together

두식의 생일을 맞아 혜진은 손수 미역국까지 끓여 두식의 집으로 달려가지만, 두식의 생일은 동네잔치가 따로 없다. 밤이 되어서야 비로소 둘만 남는데, 1년 뒤를 그리는 혜진의 말에 두식은 슬쩍 피해 답을 하고, 혜진은 어쩐지 서글퍼진다.

혜진의 대학 동기들이 공진 근처에서 열리는 세미나에 참석하러 가는 길에 윤치과에 들르고, 혜진과 두식은 엉겁결에 그들과 골프를 치러 가기로 약속한다. 혜진의 친구들 앞에서 자신의 모습을 있는 그대로 다 보여주는 두식. 하지만 동기들은 '멋진 사람 같기는 한데 결혼은 또 현실이니까'라는 말로 혜진의 마음을 뒤흔든다. 그때부터 혜진은 두식에게 언제부터 이렇게 살기로 결심한 건지, 5년 동안 대체 뭘 하며 지낸 건지 꼬치꼬치 묻지만 아무런 말이 없는 두식이다.

혜진은 잠 못 이루다 두식의 책장에서 어느 가족사진을 발견하는데, 두식은 '왜 남의 물건을 함부로 만지냐'며 예민하게 반응한다. 미래에 대한 약속도, 자신에 대한 이야기도, 뭐 하나 제대로 해주지 않는 두식을 보며 혜진은 혼란스러워지고, 두식의 눈빛 역시 슬프기만 하다. 두 사람은 처음으로 서로를 멀게 느낀다.

Hye-jin prepares seaweed soup for Du-sik's birthday, but upon arriving at his house, she finds that the townspeople are already celebrating. Finally, at night, it is just the two of them. Hye-jin wonders outloud how the two of them will be in a year from now. Du-sik is clearly uncomfortable with the conversation and changes the topic. Seeing this, Hye-jin gets mixed feelings.

Hye-jin's friends from college stop by Gongjin to attend a nearby seminar and plan to go golfing with Hye-jin and her new boyfriend. Du-sik acts as he normally does in front of Hye-jin's friends. After spending time with Du-sik, Hye-jin's friends from college tell her that Du-sik seems like a nice person, but he may not be "marriage material." Hye-jin feels conflicted hearing this and starts to ask Du-sik questions why he decided on this sort of lifestyle and what he has been doing for the five years before he returned to Gongjin. Du-sik does not say anything.

Hye-jin has trouble sleeping and decides to look through Du-sik's bookcase. She comes across a mysterious family photo. Du-sik sees this and angrily says "Why are you looking through someone else's books?" Hye-jin starts to get mixed feelings because Du-sik doesn't ever talk about himself or their future seriously. Unable to open up, Du-sik has a sad look in his eyes. For the first time, it feels as if they are becoming more distant.

드디어 우리 둘만 남았네.
홍반장, 생일 축하해.

It's finally just the two of us.
Happy birthday Chief Hong.

저희 아버지가 몸이 좀 불편하시거든요.
하반신을 못 쓰시는데 서목태가 어혈도 풀어주고
마비증에 좋대서 몇 번 달여봤어요.

조연출이 엄청 효자네.

Actually, my father is a bit ill.

He's paraplegic. I bought those beans a few times

because I heard they increase blood flow and help with paralysis.

You're such a considerate son.

홍반장이랑은 삶의 잣대가 다른 애들이야.
괜히 맘 상하게 하고 싶지 않단 말이야.

아유, 걱정하지 마. 나 그런 걸로 타격 안 받으니까.
그리고 이번 기회에 그 우물 안 개구리들한테
새로운 인생의 기준을 가르쳐주지 뭐.

They have a totally different way of life than you.
I'm just worried that you might get upset.

Geez, don't worry. I don't get affected by little things like that.
And I'll take this as an opportunity to teach your city-friends a different way of life.

우리 오빠가 원래 뭐든 잘해. 재능이 워낙 많거든.

서핑도 타고, 바리스타 자격증도 있고.

워낙 인생을 즐길 줄 아는 사람이라.

머리 좋은 사람이 몸도 잘 쓴다는 말 들어봤지?

서울대 나와서 머리도 좋은데 운동까지 잘해.

페인트도 칠하고 커피도 내리고 배도 탑니다.

현재 특정 직업을 갖고 있지 않아서요.

어디에 소속되는 대신 제 인생의 주인으로 사는 중이라.

인생에 대한 관점만 조금만 바꾸면

이렇게 살아도 충분히 행복하거든요.

인생은 한 번뿐이고, 그리고 저 이미 제가 필요한 거 다 가졌어요.

오늘 밤에 잠들 수 있는 푹신한 침대가 있고,

저한테는 튼튼한 서핑보드가 있고,

그리고 제 옆에는 제가 사랑하는 사람도 있으니까요.

My boyfriend is good at a lot of things since he has so many talents.

He surfs and he's even a certified barista.

I guess you can say he knows how to enjoy life.

You know how they say smart people also tend to be athletic, right?

He graduated from Seoul National University and he's really good at sports.

I paint, brew coffee, and navigate a boat.

I don't have a specific job right now.

Instead of having to work under someone, I choose to make my own path.

If you just change your perspective on life a little,

you'd be plenty satisfied with this sort of lifestyle.

You only live once, and I already have everything I could possibly need.

A fluffy bed to sleep in tonight,

a sturdy surfboard,

and the love of my life right next to me.

홍반장도 알고 있지?
홍반장 지난 5년에 대해 각종 소문 도는 거.
이제 나한테 말해줘도 되지 않아?
내가 얘기했잖아. 우리 사이에는 비밀이 없었으면 좋겠다고.

그냥 회사원이었어. 아주 평범한...
어차피 그만뒀는데 그게 뭐가 그렇게 중요해?

있잖아, 홍반장 다시 서울로 돌아가고 싶은 생각은 없어?

별로. 난 공진이 좋은데.
왜? 치과는 아직도 서울이 가고 싶구나?

그냥 뭐 언젠간 갈 수도 있지 않을까, 뭐 이런 생각은 하는.

그럴 수도 있겠지...

You've heard about them, right?

Of all those rumors around you about the past five years.

Isn't it okay to tell me now?

I told you, right? That I don't want any secrets between the two of us.

I was just an office worker. And a very ordinary one at that...

I quit anyways, so why does this even matter?

Chief Hong, do you have any thoughts to return to Seoul?

Not really. I like Gongjin.

Why? Do you still want to go back to Seoul?

I'm just thinking that I might want to go back to Seoul someday.

Right, that's possible...

몸에 힘이 하나도 없어.

긴장이 풀려서 그래.
고생했어. 대견하다. 장해.

나도 내가 너무 기특해.
나 너무 졸려...

우리 집으로 가자.

I don't have any energy left.

That happens after an adrenaline rush.
Good job. I'm really proud of you.

I'm also proud of myself.
I'm so tired...

Let's go to my place.

근데 누구야?
그 사진 속의 사람들?

그냥... 아는 사람.

앞으로 계속 이럴 거야?

...뭐가.

그냥 아는 사람, 그냥 회사원.
뭐 하나 얘기해주지도 않고 그냥 다 이렇게 얼버무릴 거냐고.

Who are they?

The people in the picture, I mean.

They're just... some people I know.

Are you going to keep being like this?

Like what?

"Just some people I know." "Just some office worker."

You don't tell me anything, and you keep giving me vague answers.

버킷리스트 해주겠다는 약속은 지키면서

그 온갖 것들은 다 해주면서, 왜 정작 제일 중요한 건 안 해줘?

왜 홍반장에 대한 얘기는 안 해?

난 있잖아, 홍반장이 진짜 너무 좋아.

그래서 알고 싶어.

홍반장이 어떤 삶을 살았고, 지금 무슨 생각을 하는지,

나는 홍반장이랑 내가 우리가 되는 순간을 꿈꿨는데...

왜 자꾸 내가 모르는 사람이 되려고 해...

왜 자꾸 멀어져... 왜 자꾸 낯설어져...

You've been keeping your promise about completing my bucket list,

and you agree to do all sorts of things for me,

but why won't you do the most important thing?

Why won't you open up to me?

You know, I really like you.

So I want to know everything about you.

About what kind of life you've lived, what's on your mind right now...

I've been dreaming about us becoming the kind of couple

that doesn't hide any secrets to each other.

So why do you keep trying to be someone I don't know?

Why do you keep distancing yourself? Why are you becoming a stranger?

14

당신의 약속이, 용기를 끌어낸 순간
The moment your promise gave me confidence

혜진은 절망하지만, 두식은 쉽사리 자신의 속을 내보일 수 없고. 힘들게 전화를 건 두식에게 혜진은 시간이 필요하다고 답한다. 네가 나한테 미안해지지 않기 위한 시간, 네가 나한테 솔직해지기 위한 시간. 그렇게 며칠이 지나고…

혜진은 엄마가 보내준 파김치를 들고 두식을 찾아가서, 언젠가 두식이 마음의 문을 열어준다는 확신만 있다면 기다릴 수 있으니, 안 보는 건 그만하자고, 얼굴 보며 계속 생각하라고 말한다. 혜진의 마음이 느껴지지만 아직 아무 말도 할 수 없는 두식이다.

두 사람이 싸웠다는 소문은 빠르게 마을에 퍼졌고, 사람들은 각자 혜진과 두식을 찾아 따뜻한 말 한마디를 건넨다. 그렇게 혜진, 성현, 감리의 마음에 조금씩 용기를 얻은 두식! 〈갯마을 베짱이〉 촬영 쫑파티 현장에서 혜진에게 다 끝나고 집에서 만나자는 얘기를 한다. 해야 할 말이 있다고, 아주 긴 얘기가 될 거라고. 그렇게 인생에서 가장 큰 한 발을 내딛은 두식!

그러나 그와 동시에 두식의 본명을 처음 듣게 된 조연출 도하의 얼굴이 확 굳어지고, 그는 두식의 얼굴에 곧장 주먹을 날린다.

Although Hye-jin wants to learn more about Du-sik, he can't easily open up. Hye-jin makes the hard decision to call and tell him that they should take a break. She explains he needs some time alone: "Time so that you can get over feeling sorry for me and time so that you can become honest with me." And like this, a few days pass...

After waiting a while, Hye-jin goes to Du-sik's place with some green onion kimchi sent by her step-mother. She says that if he promises to open up the door to his heart to her someday, she can wait for him. She tells him they should stop their break and that he should think it through while they're dating. Du-sik can feel Hye-jin's sincerity, but is unable to say anything in response.

Rumors that the couple fought spread throughout the town as quickly as the initial news that they were dating. The townspeople find and share words of comfort to Hye-jin and Du-sik, individually. After talking to Hye-jin, Ms. Gam-ri and Seong-hyeon, Du-sik starts to gather his courage! Du-sik tells Hye-jin to come to his place when the *The Seashore Grasshopper* after-party ends. He says he has something to tell her and that it will probably be a very long story. This may be the biggest step in Du-sik's life!

At the same time, the supporting director, Do-ha, hears Du-sik's real name for the first time. Do-ha's expression hardens and he immediately punches Du-sik in the face when he returns.

난 이제 홍반장이 누군지 모르겠어. 어떤 사람인지.

나도...
나도 모르겠어...

I don't know who you are anymore.

Me neither...
I don't know either...

나도 한 번쯤 와보고 싶었거든, 공진.
얘기를 워낙 많이 들어서.

그래? 누구한테?

아는 사람. 여기가 고향이래.

I wanted to come to Gongjin at least once.

I've heard so much about it.

Really? From who?

Just someone I know. He said this is his hometown.

어차피 홍반장 지금 나 만나도 미안하단 말밖에 안 할 거잖아.

지금 벌써 한 번 했고.

내 생각엔, 아무래도 우리 시간이 좀 필요한 것 같아.

이별 전에 의례적으로 하는 말 아니야.

나 홍반장이랑 헤어지기 싫거든.

그냥 시간이 좀 필요해 보여서.

홍반장이 나한테 미안해지지 않기 위한 시간.

나한테 솔직해질 수 있을 만큼의 시간.

우리 이렇게는 안 될 것 같아.

우리 조금 시간을 갖고 천천히 생각해보자.

앞으로 어떻게 하면 좋을지, 어떻게 하고 싶은지.

Even if I meet you now, you'll just keep apologizing.

Just like you did right now.

I think we need some time apart.

I'm not saying this as a formality before breaking up,

because I don't want to break up with you.

It just looks like you need some time.

Time so that you can get over feeling sorry for me

and time so that you can become honest with me.

I don't think we can go on like this.

Let's take it slowly and carefully think this through.

About what we should do from now and what we both want.

홍반장 아직 나한테 할 말 없잖아...

You don't have anything to say to me, right?

홍반장이 나한테 언젠가 마음을 열어준다는 확신만 준다면,
나 기다릴 수 있을 것 같아.
그냥 당장 뭐 어쩌자고 하는 거 아니야.
그냥 내가 바라는 건 여지였어.
홍반장의 내일에 내가 조금은 포함되어 있는지,
그리고 우리가 앞으로 함께할 가능성이 있는지,
그게 궁금했었던 것 같아.
나는 결론 내렸지만, 홍반장한테는 추가 시간을 줄게.
근데 안 보는 건 그만하자.
보면서 생각해. 그냥 보면서 계속 생각해.
근데 너무 오래 기다리게 하지는 마.

If you can promise me that you'll open the door to your heart to me one day,
I think I could wait.
I'm not saying you to do something this second.
I just want to know if there's the possibility
that I'll be a part of the future you envision.
And whether you see a future where we're together?
I think that's all I wanted to know.
I've made up my mind, but I'll give you some more time.
But let's end our break.
Think about it while we date. Take your time thinking about it while we're together.
Just... don't make me wait too long.

모두 고생하셨습니다!

Good work everyone!

홍반장님. 저도 여러모로 신세 많이 졌어요.
그때 주신 약재, 아빠가 그거 먹고 컨디션 한결 좋아지셨대요.

다행이네. 내가 올라가기 전에 한 번 더 챙겨줄게.

Chief Hong, I'm also grateful to you for many things.
My father's condition has gotten better after eating the medicinal herb you gave him.

That's good to hear. I'll get you some more before you go to Seoul.

두식아, 너 저 치과선상이랑 싸웠지?

얼른 가서 잘못했다 하고 끈안나줘.

너 치과선상 그러다 지풀에 지체갖고 나가떨어지믄 우태할라 그러니.

힘들게 맺은 인연, 끙케나가지 않게 니가 잘해야 대.

두식아... 나는 니 옆에 치과선상이 있는 거 차암 좋다.

니 사람들한테 잘하는 것도 좋지만, 너를 위해 살아야 해.

마수운 것도 마이 먹고 행복해야 대.

니가 행복해야 내도 행복하고 또 치과선상도 행복할 기야.

여 공진 사람들 마카 다 그렇게 생각할 거라니.

할머니. 정말 내가 그래도 될까?

아, 당연하지. 말이라고 하나?

그간 동동거리며 사느라고 고생했싸.

인제는 다리 쭉 펴고 편히 살아라.

Du-sik, ya had an argument with the dentist, right?

Hurry up and go tell'er that yer sorry and give'er a hug.

What're ya gonna do if the dentist gets tired of waiting and gives up on ya?

This kinda relationship is hard ta come by, so ya have'ta do your best to not lose it.

Du-sik... I'm so glad that ya have the dentist by yer side now.

Yer selflessness is good, but ya have'ta learn to live for ya'self too.

Ya should eat lotsa good food and be happy.

If yer happy, I will be happy and the dentist will be happy.

I'm sure everyone in Gongjin would agree.

Grandma, is it really okay if I do that?

Gosh, of course. Don't be ridiculous.

I know ya had a hard time these past years.

Now ya should live comfortably and only think about ya'self.

여러분들의 배려 덕분에 촬영 잘 마칠 수 있었습니다.
오며 가며 웃어주시고 덕담해주시고.
감사함 절대 잊지 않겠습니다!
방송 꼭 봐주시고요, 감사합니다.

Thanks to everyone's kindness and generosity, we were able to finish the shoot smoothly.
I will never forget your smiles and words of encouragement!
Please watch the show when it airs. Thank you!

오늘 꼭 할 말이 있어.
어쩌면 아주 긴 얘기가 될 거야.
그래도 들어줄래?

There's something I have to tell you today.
It'll probably be a very long story.
Will you still hear it?

홍반장님,
이름 홍두식 맞아요?

Chief Hong,
is your name really Hong Du-sik?

15

당신의 슬픔이, 봄을 맞이한 순간
The moment your sadness meets spring

드디어 밝혀지는 두식의 과거! 힘이 되고 싶은 혜진이지만, 두식은 모든 게 다 자신 때문이라며 차갑게 돌아선다.

홍반장이 없으니 공진은 어느 것 하나 제대로 돌아가지 않고, 어둠 속에 갇힌 두식을 위해 감리는 매일 따뜻한 끼니를 손수 챙긴다. 하지만 한 술도 뜨지 않는 두식. 걱정스러운 마음에 집으로 찾아간 혜진에게 두식은 힘겹게 자신의 과거 이야기를 시작한다. 대학 선배인 정우와 어떻게 알게 됐으며, 펀드매니저 일은 왜 하게 됐는지. 도하 아버지가 자살 기도한 이유와 정우 형이 죽던 날의 기억까지. 그날 밤, 두식은 혜진의 품에 안겨 처음으로 온갖 감정을 토해낸다. 그리고 다음 날, 도하와도 서툴지만 서로의 진심을 나누며 오해를 푼다.

한껏 앓은 두식은 혜진과 함께 정우를 만나러 가는 길에 정우의 아내인 선아와 그들의 아이 하랑과 마주친다. 죄책감을 안고 살아가던 두식은 그들로부터 따뜻한 위로를 받고 그제야 편히 웃을 수 있게 된다.

한편, 감리, 맏이, 숙자가 함께 누워 잠든 방. 요란하게 자는 숙자 때문에 잠에서 깬 맏이는 이상한 기분이 들어 감리의 숨소리를 들어보는데, 너무나 고요하다. 평온한 표정으로 길고 긴 잠에 든 감리. 맏이는 감리에게 마지막 인사를 건넨다.

Du-sik finally opens up about his past! Du-sik believes that everything is his fault and nothing Hye-jin says is able to change his mind.

With Du-sik staying locked in his house, nothing in Gongjin seems to run smoothly. Ms. Gam-ri prepares warm meals for Du-sik everyday. Worried about Du-sik, Hye-jin goes to his place. Although his past is difficult to talk about, Du-sik musters the courage and begins to tell Hye-jin about it. He talks about how he got to know Jeong-u, who was his upperclassman in college, why he began to work as a fund manager, the reason Do-ha's father attempted suicide, and his memory of the day that Jeong-u died. That night in Hye-jin's arms, Du-sik shares his deepest emotions for the first time. And the next day, Do-ha visits Du-sik and the two are able to resolve their misunderstandings.

After being sick for a long time, Du-sik finally goes to see Jeong-u with Hye-jin. On their way, Du-sik meets Jeong-u's wife and son. Du-sik, who has been living with the guilt of ruining this family, receives warm comfort from Jeong-u's wife and son and, at last, Du-sik is able to smile comfortably.

Meanwhile, Ms. Gam-ri, Mat-i, and Suk-ja are sleeping together in a room. Mat-i wakes up to Suk-ja moving in her sleep. Mat-i has a strange feeling and listens to Gam-ri's calm breathing. Then, with a very serene expression, Ms. Gam-ri passes away. Mat-i says her last farewell to Ms. Gam-ri.

너 알지, 우리 아버지? 또 도망가?

너 이런 데서 숨어서 잘도 살았네.

세상 좋은 사람인 척 가면이나 쓰고.

두 발 뻗고 잠이 와?

You know my father, right? You're running away again?

So, this is where you've been hiding this whole time,

pretending to be a good person and everything.

How do you even sleep at night?

따라오지 마.
네가 들은 말 전부 사실이야.
도하 아버지 그렇게 만든 사람 나 맞아.
그뿐만이 아니라 네가 본 사진 속 가족도 내가 망가뜨렸어.
내가... 형을 죽였어.

Don't follow me.

Everything you just heard is the truth.

I'm the one who made Do-ha's father like that.

Not only that, but I also destroyed the family in the photo you saw.

I... killed him.

밥 안 먹었어? 왜 이렇게 말랐어...
나 아직 시간 준다는 거 유효해.
나 기다릴 수 있어.

Did you not eat yet? You look thinner...
What I said about giving you some time is still valid.
I can wait.

내 얘기... 듣고 가.
내가 할 말이... 있다고 했잖아.

Before you go... hear my story.
I told you... that I have something to say.

형이 있었어...
나는 신입생, 형은 복학생이었고.
한 방에서 지내니까 자동으로 친해지더라고.
매일 같이 술 마시고, 해장하고 또 술 마시고.
할아버지 기일에는 같이 제사도 지내고.
형 때문에 알았어. 나한테도 친형이 있으면 이런 느낌이겠구나.
사실은 회사도 형 따라 들어간 거야. 형이 펀드매니저였거든.

I had a close friend...

I was a freshman and he was a returning student.

We naturally became close because we were roommates.

We'd go out drinking everyday, get over out hangovers, and then go drinking again.

We even held my grandpa's memorial service together.

Thanks to him I realized what it would feel like to have an older brother.

He even convinced me to work at that company. He was the fund manager there, you see.

시작해보니까 의외로 일이 재밌었어.
적성에도 맞고 돈도 잘 벌고
새로운 사람들도 많이 만나고.
도하 아버지도 거기서 알게 됐어.

Thinking back on it, the work was surprisingly fun.
It suited me and it made me good money.
I got to meet a lot of new people.
That's where I met Do-ha's father.

어느 날 아저씨가 내 펀드에 가입하고 싶다고 하시는 거야.
내가 운용하는 펀드들이 수익률이 꽤 높았거든.
리스크가 크니까 처음엔 말렸지.
근데 워낙 간곡히 부탁을 하시더라고.
그런데... 일이 터졌어.

One day he told me that he wanted to subscribe to my fund,
since the trust funds I managed had pretty high returns.
I tried to stop him at first because of the high risks.
But he kept asking me.
Then... things went wrong.

그 소식 들으셨어요?
우리 회사 경비 아저씨, 자살 기도했대요.

Have you heard the news?
Our security guard attempted suicide.

내가 운전할게.
너 지금 이 상태로 운전하면 안 돼, 내려.
두식아, 내려.

I'll drive.
You can't drive in this state. Move.
Du-sik, get out.

울어도 돼, 홍반장.
홍반장도 힘들었을 거 아니야.
힘든 거 꾹꾹 눌러왔을 거 아니야.
심장에 모래주머니 매달고 살았을 거야.
나한테는 슬프다고 해도 돼.
나한테는 아프다고 해도 돼, 홍반장.
울어도 돼...
울어도 돼...

It's okay to cry Chief Hong.

It must've been so hard for you too.

Suppressing your pain deep down like this,

it must've been hard to live with such a heavy heart.

You don't have to hide that you're sad when you're with me.

You can tell me if you're hurting.

You can cry...

You can cry...

항상 이상하다고 생각했어.
아빠 그렇게 되고 나서,
우리 집은 분명히 풍비박산이 났어야 됐는데
오히려 이사를 갔거든. 아파트로.
엄마가 그러는 거야.
학자금 대출 다 갚았으니까, 넌 취업 준비만 열심히 하라고.
아빠 병원비도 걱정하지 말라고.
엄마는 보험금 덕분이랬지만 그게 말이 안 되잖아.
내가 우리 집 형편 뻔히 아는데.
혹시 당신이었어?

I always thought it was weird.

After what happened to my dad,

I thought my family would become dirt-poor,

but instead we moved to an apartment.

My mom said that I should focus on getting a job,

since my student loans have been paid off.

She even told me not to worry about dad's hospital bills.

Mom said that it was all because of our insurance,

but that didn't make sense.

I know my family's financial situation.

Was it you?

당신 잘못 아니야, 내가 아닌 거 아는데.
나도 누구 원망할 사람이 필요했어. 그냥.

It's not your fault. I know that.
I just needed someone to blame.

나 면접 보러 갈 때 형이 사준 옷이야.

의미 있는 옷이네. 형이 좋아하시겠다.

Jeong-u bought this suit for me for my job interview.

How meaningful. Jeong-u would love this.

두식아,
나는 이제 더는 너를 원망하지 않아.
그러니까 너도 이제 그만 너 자신을 용서해줘.

Du-sik,
I don't blame you anymore.
So, you should forgive yourself as well.

웃으니까 좋네...
그렇게 웃어.
내가 이렇게 웃어도 되나,
내가 이렇게 행복해도 되나,
그렇게 너무 생각하지 말고, 웃어.

It's nice to see you smile...
Keep smiling like that.
Don't overthink about
whether you can smile like this,
or whether you can be happy like this. Just smile.

혜진아.

나 사실은 그때 죽으려고 그랬어.

나는 살았는데 형은 잘못됐다는 얘기 듣고

병원에서 그대로 뛰쳐나갔어.

하염없이 걷다가 한강 다리에서 멈춰 섰는데,

그런 생각이 들더라.

여기서 생을 끝내자.

그럼 이 물이 돌고 돌아 바다에 닿겠지.

그럼 부모님도 만날 수 있으려나.

Hye-jin.

To be honest, I was going to kill myself then.

When I heard that Jeong-u had died, I ran out of the hospital.

I was walking aimlessly and then I found myself at a bridge

on the Han River.

That's when I thought,

I should just end my life here.

Then this river water will take me to the ocean.

And then I might be able to meet my parents again.

두식아.
내거 서울으 완데 혹시 볼 수 있나?
니 조와하는 반찬도 싸 왔다니.
얼굴 까먹겠싸.
내 니 마이 보고 숲다.

Du-sik.
I just came ta Seoul. Can I see ya?
I brought yer favorite side dishes.
It's been so long, I might forget yer face.
I miss ya lots.

띄어쓰기도 맞춤법도 다 틀린 그 문자가 나를 붙잡았어.
죽기로 결심한 그날, 감리씨가 공진이 나를 살렸어.

Even with all of its spelling and grammar mistakes,
Ms. Gam-ri's text touched me.
That day, when I made the decision to die,
Ms. Gam-ri and Gongjin saved me.

이제 내 얘기는 이걸로 끝이야.
오래 기다리게 해서 미안해.

고마워.
계속 미완결인 줄 알았는데,
이렇게 용기 내서 얘기해줘서 너무 고마워.

전부 너한테 배운 거야. 너 없었으면 못 했을 거야.
그날 혜진이 너도 나한테 뭐 할 말 있다고 하지 않았어?
얘기하기 곤란하면 안 해도 돼.
이번에는 내가 기다려줄게.
네가 나한테 그랬던 것처럼.

So that's the end of my story.
I'm sorry I made you wait so long.

Thank you.
I was worried you might never open up.
So, thank you for taking the courage to tell me. Really.

I learned it from you. I could've never done this without you.
But that day, didn't you have something to tell me too?
You don't have to tell me now if it's hard to say.
This time, I'll be the one to wait for you.
Just like you did for me.

나 서울 안 가고 싶어. 여기 있을 거야.
나 여기서 해야 될 일이 너무 많거든.
그리고 마지막으로 홍반장이 여기 있잖아.

고마워. 고마워, 혜진아.

I don't want to go to Seoul. I'm gonna stay here.

There's so many things I have to do here.

And lastly, you're here.

Thank you. Thank you, Hye-jin.

16

우리의 인생이, 모두와 춤추는 순간
The moment everyone dances together

감리의 장례식. 따뜻한 공진 사람들의 품에서 감리는 먼 소풍을 떠난다. 장례식을 치른 후 혜진은 두식의 집에 들렀다가, 옥수수 소쿠리 속에 감리가 넣어둔 편지 한 장을 발견한다. 두식을 향한 감리의 애틋한 마음이 담긴 편지. 인생에서 수많은 이별을 경험하고도 매번 참기만 했던 두식은 그날 처음으로 있는 그대로의 감정을 쏟아내며 한없이 운다.

한 달 뒤, 혜진이 서울로 2박 3일 학회를 떠나자 두식은 익숙하기만 했던 혼자의 삶이 생경하고 외롭게 느껴진다. 집 안 여기저기에서 혜진의 모습이 보였다 사라질 때면 보고 싶은 마음이 더욱 간절해지고, 이는 혜진도 마찬가지다. 하루라도 빨리 홍반장의 가족이 되어주고 싶다. 공진으로 돌아온 혜진은 두식에게 프러포즈를 하는데, 두식은 자신도 프러포즈를 하려 했다며 당황하고, 혜진은 프러포즈 이어달리기를 하라며 주먹 불끈 파이팅을 외친다. 서로에게 청혼하는 모습도 티키타카 사랑스러운 두 사람.

어느 멋진 날. 혜진과 두식은 공진 바다를 배경으로 웨딩 사진 촬영에 나서고 어느덧 잔뜩 모인 공진 사람들은 둘을 연신 따라다니며 도움을 주는데, 방해인지 도움인지 영 모르겠다. 하지만 하나 확실한 건 모두의 웃음이 공진 햇살보다도 밝고 공진 바다만큼이나 시원하다는 사실이 아닐까!

It's the day of Ms. Gam-ri's funeral. The warm people of Gongjin send Ms. Gam-ri on her a far away picnic. After the funeral, Hye-jin goes to Du-sik's house and finds a letter that Ms. Gam-ri left for Du-sik in the basket of corn. Du-sik reads Ms. Gam-ri's affectionate letter. Du-sik, who has experienced many deaths in his life, pours out all his emotions and cries his eyes out for the first time.

One month later, Hye-jin leaves for a three-day seminar in Seoul and Du-sik is suddenly all alone. Even though he was used to being alone, he now finds it unfamiliar and lonely. Everywhere he looks in the house reminds him of Hye-jin, which only makes him miss her more. In Seoul, Hye-jin also misses him a lot. She decides that she wants to be a family with him and when she returns to Gongjin, she proposes right away. Du-sik is taken aback because he was also planning to propose today. Hye-jin suggests he think of it as a relay race and encourages him to say his proposal. The two look very happy and lovely proposing to each other.

One beautiful day, Hye-jin and Du-sik are taking wedding photos on the beach. Soon, many Gongjin townspeople gather around them and it is hard to tell if they're being helpful or a disturbance. Nonetheless, on this day, everyone's laughter is brighter than the sun and clearer than the Gongjin sea!

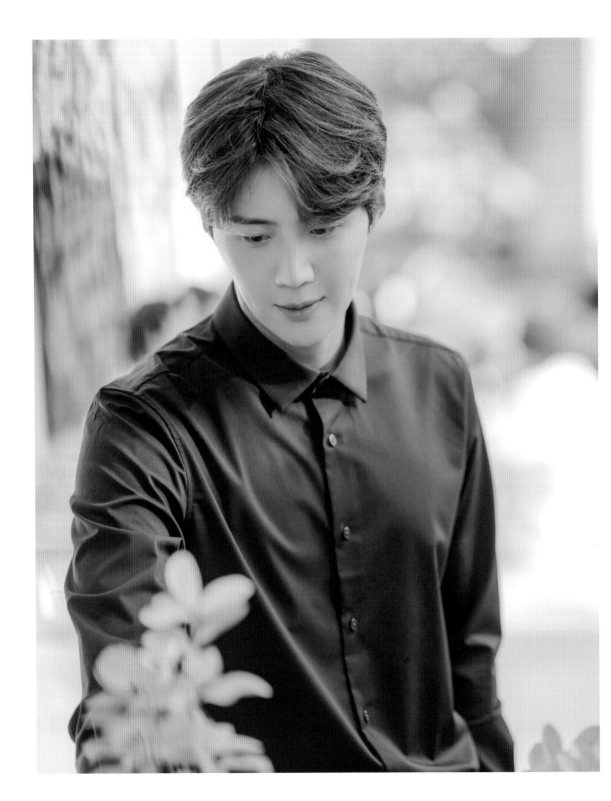

이 사진들은 뭐야?

예전에 감리씨가 계장님 아들 결혼식에서
포토테이블을 보더니 나한테 그러시더라고.
나중에 내 장례식 때도 이런 거 하나 있었으면 좋겠다니.
그래서 내가 그게 무슨 소리냐고 물어보니까
앞으로 남은 제일 성대한 잔치가 장례식일 텐데
다들 웃고 떠들고 실컷 놀다 갔으면 좋겠대.
좋은 데로 갔을 테니까 감재적이나 부쳐 먹고 막걸리나 실컷 마시래.
그래서 우리 다 같이 감리씨 마지막 소원 들어드리는 중이야.

What are these photos?

A while ago, Ms. Gam-ri saw a photo table set up at our neighbor's son's wedding,
and she told me that she'd like one of those at her own funeral.
When I asked her what she was talking about,
she said that the biggest event left for her was her funeral.
She wanted it to be festive and for her guests to have a good time chatting and laughing.
She said to eat potato jeon and drink makgeolli for her since she'll have gone to a good place.
So, we're making her final wishes come true right now.

두식아. 나 어머니 얼굴이 잘 기억이 안 난다.
하루 종일 영정사진 보고 있는데도 왜 이렇게 딴 사람 같냐.
나는 엄마가... 내 옆에 아주 오래 있을 줄 알았어.
그래서 늘 다음에 보면 되지, 다음에 보면 되지 그랬는데.
이젠 다음이 없네.

Du-sik, I can't remember my mother's face that well.
Even though I've been looking at her portrait photo all day,
she seems like a different person.
I thought... my mom would stay alive for a very long time.
So, I kept saying I can see her "next time" and kept putting off seeing her.
But now there's no next time.

나는 지금이 참 좋다.
나이 먹은 만큼 마수운 것도 마이 먹어봤고 좋은 풍경도 마이 봤고
사람들도 얻었잖나. 그거보다 더 행복한 게 어디 있겠나?

성님은 행복해?

으응. 행복하제.
텔레비전에도 나가봤고 동네 노래자랑에서 노래도 해봤고
니들과 또 이래 지껄이고 있으니 을매나 재미지나. 그뿐이나?
오늘 노을이 참 고왔싸. 즈냑에 먹은 오징어도 마수웠고.
잘 둘러보라니. 마카 귀한 것투성이야.
나는 매일이 소풍 가기 전날인 것 같다니.

I really like ma age.

In ma long life, I got to try many delicious foods, see beautiful sceneries,

and met wonderful folks. How could I be happier than this?

Are you happy?

Of course, I'm happy.

I gotta appear on a TV show, sing on a stage,

and now I'm chatting with ya'll. I'm havin' lotsa fun. That's not all.

Today's sunset was so beautiful and the squid I had for dinner was delicious.

Take a good look around and ya will realize that there are many precious things surrounding ya.

For me, everyday feels so exciting. Almost as if I'm going on a picnic the next day.

잘 자오. 예쁜 소풍, 먼저 가서 기다려요.

Sleep well. Go ahead to ya pretty picnic first and wait for me.

있잖아.
사랑하는 사람을 잃었을 때는 충분히 아파해야 된대.
안 그러면 슬픔이 온몸을 타고 돌아다니다가
나중에 크게 터져버리거든.

You know,
they say when you lose someone you love,
you should take your time grieving.
Otherwise, the sadness will travel all around your body
and explode later.

두식아. 밥 먹으라니.

아무리 힘든 일이 있싸도 밥은 꼭 먹어이 대.

언나 적부터 가슴에 멍이 개락인 너인테, 내거 해줄 기 밥밖에 없었싸.

그 밥 먹고 키가 크다맣게 됐으니, 그기 을매나 기특했나 몰라.

두식아. 니가 알쿼준 말 기억하나?

부모가 진짜 자슥을 위하는 일은 아프지 않는 거랬제.

부모 맘도 똑같다니. 자슥이 아프믄 억장이 무너져...

두식이 니는 내인테 아들이고, 손주야...

그기르 절대 잊으면은 안 돼.

두식아. 사람은 마카 사람들 사이에서 살아야 대.

가끔은 사는 기 묵직할 끼야. 그래도 사람들 사이에 있으믄 있잖아?

니가 내르 업어준 것처럼, 분명 누가 니르 업어줄 꺼야.

그래니 두식아. 혼저 가두케 있지 말고 할머이 밥 먹고 얼릉 나오라니, 응.

Du-sik. Ya gotta eat.

No matter how hard yer life gets, ya still have'ta eat.

The only thing I could do for ya,

who has been living with a broken heart for so long, was to cook for ya.

Seeing ya eat my food and grow so tall made me so proud.

Du-sik, do ya remember what ya said to me?

Ya said the best thing a parent could do for their child is staying healthy.

It's the same for parents. Our hearts break when our children are in pain...

Du-sik, to me, ya are ma son and ma grandson...

Don't ya ever forget that.

Du-sik, people should live surrounded by other folks.

Life may be rough sometimes, but if ya surround ya'self with good folks,

just like ya did for me, there will always be someone ya can lean on.

So Du-sik, don't stay locked up alone in yer house,

but eat ma food and then hurry and come out.

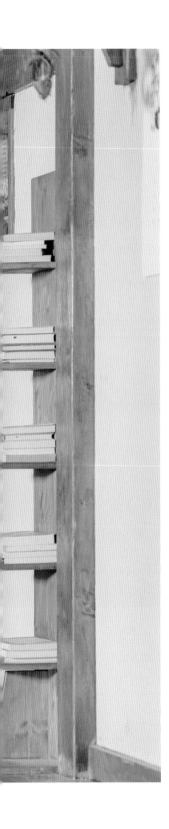

우리는 그날 감리 할머니와 뒤늦은 안녕을 했다.
인생에서 수많은 죽음을 경험하고도 그저 참기만 했을 뿐,
단 한 번도 충분히 슬퍼하지 못했던 그는...
처음으로 오래 울었다.
그리고 사람들 역시 저마다의 방식으로 할머니를 애도하고 있었다.
그 속에서 우리는 깨달았다.
소중한 기억이 있는 한,
존재는 결코 사라지지 않는다는 것을.

That day, we gave our belated farewells to Ms. Gam-ri.
Even though he's experienced so many deaths in his life,
he's always kept his sadness bottled up
and never allowed himself to grieve properly.
For the first time, he cried for a long time.
Others were also mourning the loss of Ms. Gam-ri in their
own ways.
Through these difficult times, we realized
that as long as we keep our precious memories of them,
our loved ones are never truly gone.

누가 보면 서울로 이사 가는 줄 알겠네.
야, 윤혜진. 너는 2박 3일 학회 가면서 뭔 짐을 이렇게 많이 싸냐?

Seeing your luggage, people would think that you're moving to Seoul.

Hey Yoon Hye-jin, why are you packing so much for a three-day seminar?

나 진짜 며칠을 어떻게 안 본담.

안 되겠다. 홍반장 서울 같이 가자.

캐리어에 넣어가고 싶다.

How am I going to live without seeing you for a few days?

It's impossible. Let's go to Seoul together.

I want to take you in my suitcase.

아오, 나도 이제 물린다, 쟤들.

God, I'm getting sick of them.

되게 보고 싶네.

I really miss her.

현관에 우리 신발이 늘 나란히 놓여져 있으면 좋겠어.
외롭지 않게.
홍반장. 나랑 결혼해줄래?

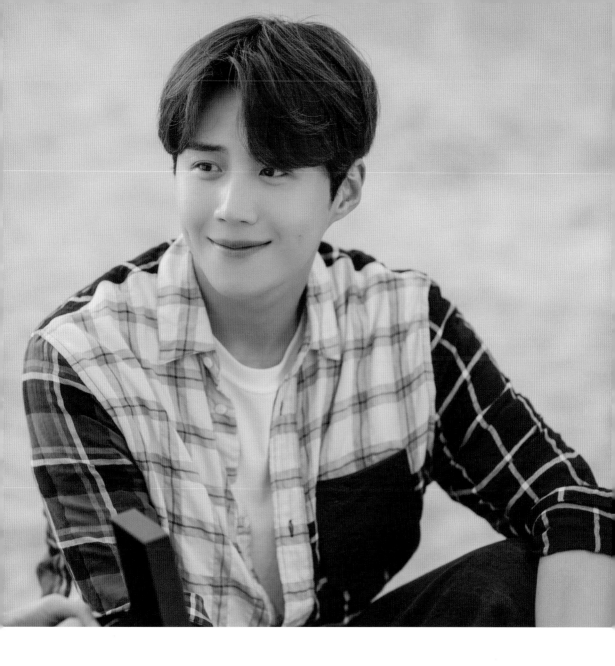

I hope our shoes can always be side-by-side on the porch.

So that they're never lonely.

Chief Hong, will you marry me?

나도 오늘 프러포즈 하려고 그랬단 말이야.
내가 먼저 하려고 했는데,
내가 진짜 한참 전부터 준비한 건데.

그러면 지금부터 홍반장이 해.
내가 바톤터치 할게.
이어달리기라고 생각하자. 홍반장이 마지막 주자야.
결승선에 골인하면 돼!
할 수 있어, 파이팅.

I was planning to propose to you today too.
I wanted to do it first.
Even though I've been preparing for a long time.

Alright then, starting now you take the lead.
I'm handing the baton to you.
Think of it as a relay race. You're the final runner.
You just need to get to the finish line!
You can do it! Good luck!

그날 바다에서 어떤 여자를 봤어.
한참을 앉아 있는데 눈빛이 너무 슬퍼 보이는 거야.
근데 그게 자꾸 맘에 밟혔어.
그래서 계속 눈길이 가더라고.
근데 그 여자를... 이렇게 사랑하게 될 줄 몰랐네.

That day I saw a random woman on the beach.

She sat there for a long time with a sad look in her eyes.

And I couldn't get that scene out of my mind,

so my eyes kept being drawn to her.

But to think... that I'd end up falling in love with her this much.

현관에는 신발 두 켤레,
또 화장실엔 칫솔 두 개,
부엌에는 앞치마 두 벌.
뭐든지 다 한 쌍씩 놓자.
그런 집에서 오늘을, 내일을,
그리고 모든 시간을 나랑 함께 살자.

Two shoes on the porch,

two toothbrushes in the bathroom,

and two aprons in the kitchen,

We'll get everything in pairs.

And in that house, let's spend today, tomorrow,

and all of our time together.

사랑해.

나도.

I love you.

Me too.

결혼 생활에 필요한 공동 규약을 만들고 있었어.
내가 계획형 인간인데 좀 급진파야.

I'm making a contract for our married life.
I like to plan well ahead. Sometimes to a little extreme extent.

언제까지 홍반장이라고 부를 거야?
나처럼 이름을 부르든가.

두식씨. 두식아.
...오빠! ...오빠? 오빠, 오빠.

아 이상하다. 아직도 소름이 돋냐.

뭐라고 부를까. 자기?

어, 나 그거 좋은데?
원래 자기가 나를 가리키는 말이잖아.
네가 그렇게 불러주니까
내가 너고 네가 내가 돼서 불러주는 기분이야.

How long are you going to keep calling me Chief Hong?
Call me by my name, like I do for you.

Mr. Du-sik. Du-sik.
...Oppa! ...Oppa? Oppa, oppa.

That feels weird. I still have goosebumps.

What should I call you? Jagi*?

Ohh, I like that sound of that.
Because jagi also means self,
when you call me jagi it kinda feels like
I'm you and you're me.

* jagi: In Korean, jagi means myself but it can also be used to call your lover (similar to "darling" or "honey").

나 오늘 집에 안 갈 거야.

보낼 생각도 없었거든?

I'm not going home tonight.

I wasn't planning on letting you go anyways.

배고프지? 내가 토스트 만들었는데. 이것 좀 먹어봐.
왜? 먹기 싫어?

아니, 나 손이 없어. 아직 옷을 못 입었거든...

그대로 있어. 내가 먹여줄게.

You're hungry, right? I made toast. Try some of this.
Why? You don't want to eat?

No, I just can't use my hands right now because I didn't get dressed yet...

Stay still. I'll feed you.

저희 결혼해요!

We're getting married!

우리 진짜 결혼해!

We're really getting married!

갈까?

아임 레디!

Should we go?

I'm ready!

아유, 너무 이쁘다.
이모님 알지? 내가 그거 해줄게.
뭘 사양하고 그래.
미안해하지 않아도 돼.

Gosh, you two look great!
You need a helper, right? I'll do it.
No need to decline.
Don't be sorry.

내가 셋 하면 뛰는 거야.
하나... 둘... 셋!

We're going to escape on three.

One... Two... Three!

449

늘 이렇게 잔잔하지만은 않을 거야.
풍랑도 있을 거고.
태풍이 불어닥치는 날도 있을 거야.

I'm sure the sea won't always be this calm.

We'll face wind and turbulent waves.

And there'll be typhoon days too.

비 좀 맞으면 어때?
바람 좀 불면 어때?
우리가 같이 한배를 탔는데.

So what if we get soaked in a little rain?

And who cares if there's a little wind?

All that matters is that we're riding the same boat together.

여보세요?
어? 넘어지셨다고?

Hello?
What? She fell?

여보세요?
입안이 찢어지셨다고요?

Hello?
She tore the inside of her mouth?

Behind story

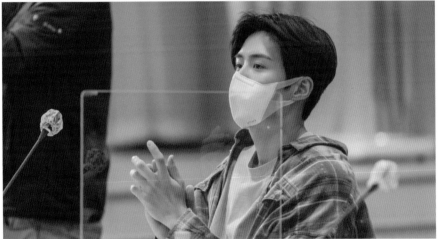

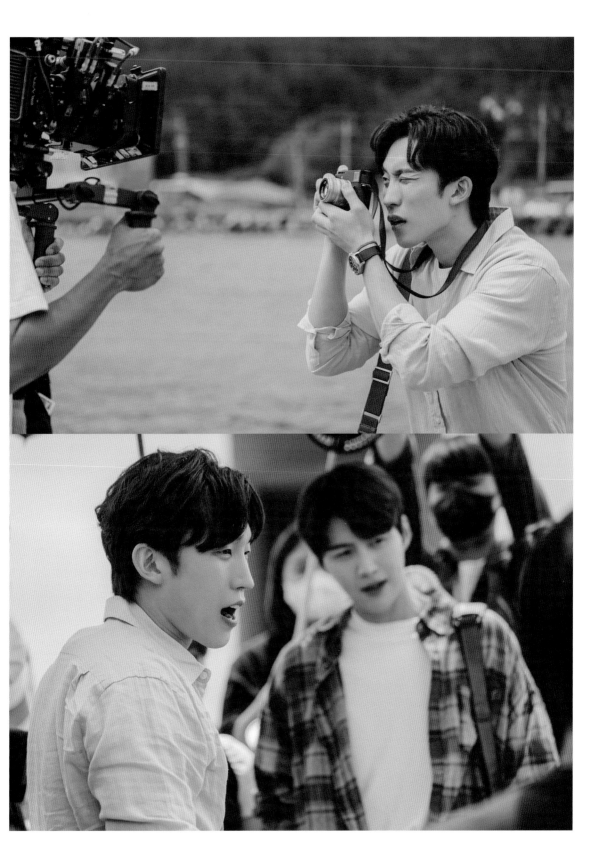

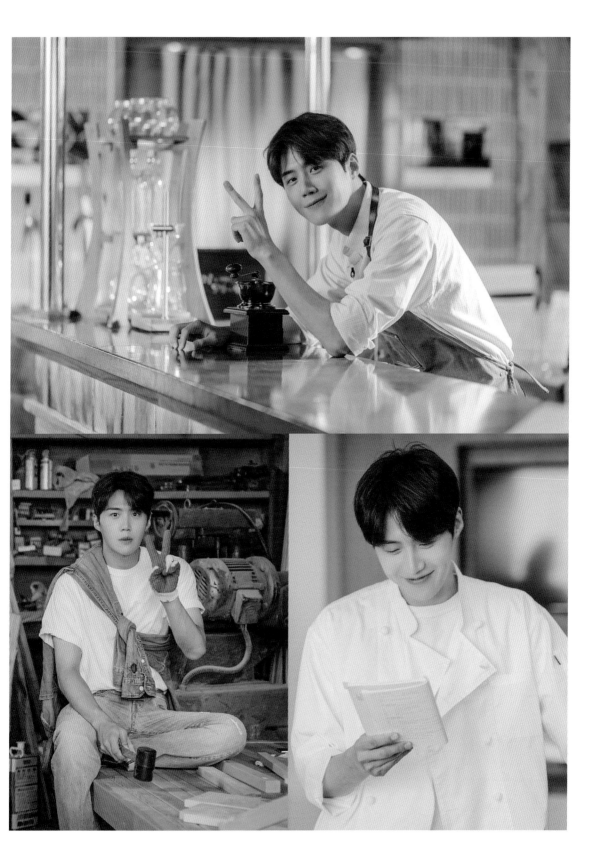

DRAMA STAFF

기획 tvN 스튜디오드래곤
제작 지티스트
극본 신하은
연출 유제원
출연 신민아 김선호 이상이 외

스튜디오드래곤

기획 김영규 | **책임프로듀서** 조문주 | **프로듀서** 이상희 | **사업총괄** 유봉열 | **콘텐츠사업** 김주연 전슬기 | **IP사업** 임하영 이주혜 | **마케팅 대행** [마코] 김경석 안윤수 오영교 | **콘텐츠운영** 안지현 이미정 이보현 | **콘텐츠전략** 최보연 허주미 최민영 최수정 | **사업전략담당** 이기혁 | **사업전략** 이혜미 김송래 정선화 박예은 이힘찬 | **법무** 이규상 문주예 오혜진 | **홍보** 김찬혁 원설란 | **심의** 김미라

tvN

tvN총괄기획 김제현 | **tvN IP사업총괄** 김종훈 | **마케팅&디자인총괄** 김재인 | **마케팅** 김민재 임성빈 전수련 유지수 | **콘텐츠운영** 박정연 진종욱 강상백 이효연 | **드라마운영** 이상화 이하림 서영평 | **운행** 손지영 박하린 최윤정 최서영 이예은 이송이 정유민 이형규 | **편성제작** 유정민 최수빈 | **사업전략총괄** 김성석 | **제작관리** 김보라 정다운 한득연 | **방송운영책임** 홍주리 | **심의** 박재익 이지나 장강민 김소영 김아름 | **홍보총괄** 장영석 | **홍보책임** 안미현 | **홍보진행** 이상훈 장혜진 | **홍보대행** [와이키키] 윤지민 김보라 | **온라인서비스** 양희선 신다애 김은지 문지윤 이슬 | **소셜콘텐츠기획제작** 김진주 이정용 권준희 정예린 | **법률검토** 정동완 박지혜 | **SNS운영** 민소현 김단

지티스트

제작 이동규 | **제작총괄** 박수영 | **제작프로듀서** 김형우 임한준 김병건 | **라인프로듀서** 이승준 권은지 | **제작행정** 하성애 홍수경

촬영 박정훈(CGK) 이정원 전홍규 하진경 | **포커스플로어** 유성철 김상곤 조진우 이지인 | **촬영팀** 류승규 김성민 조연정 이율기 김효찬 박성우 이성모 윤승원 이승은 이충민 이현우 조희주 | **드론** [D.X.F] 이승규 박진국 | **FPV** 김영중 | **DIT** [BASE] 고동균 | **DIT팀** 장찬수 김성수 노종탁 이슬히 | **조명** [투에스엠 라이팅컴퍼니] 김보현 [미스터 손씨] 손창영 | **조명1st** 권인호 장한별 | **조명팀** 강경근 최승환 이은환 이성민 정예주 김민철 김건우 진은비 강영훈 | **발전차** [G.LINE] 이인교 [수] 김인수 | **그립** [이모션그립] 최용재 나성식 | **그립팀** 강진환 한철웅 정대룡 박우현 | **동시녹음** [얌미디어] 이동기 김정옥 | **붐오퍼레이터** 김진웅 공훈력 | **라인** 윤하림 임영진 | **무술감독** [액션드래곤] 이종연 최태정 | **보조출연** [케이에스콘텐츠] 이경수 박동화 | **캐스팅디렉터** [티아이] 정치인 민정섭 | **아역캐스팅** [티아이] 노태민 최학수 | **미술** [꾸러기딱지미술상회] | **미술감독** 류선광 곽재식 | **미술팀장** 남미지 | **미술팀** 신원진, 백시은, 권지원 | **세트** [가김지인] 김민수 | **제작팀장** 한용수 | **작화팀장** 나병진 | **마감팀장** 홍도명 | **포항 제작팀장** 손수범 | **포항 작화팀장** 이명준 | **포항 진행팀** 문종화 윤종훈 | **소품** [공간] 최병욱 | **인테리어스타일리스트** 전승민 | **소품팀장** 김지호 | **소품팀** 이슬기 권우진 조민수 | **소품지원** 전세광 박경화 이미지 | **소품차량** 임병조 | **의상** [가온] 이수진 | **의상팀** 정다이 봉선우 이경신 | **의상차** 백승석 강승관 | **분장미용** [레나타] 임경란 | **분장미용팀장** 최연지 | **분장미용팀** 송청수 이세린 김수정 | **특수분장** [캐스트] 이주엔 | **특수효과** [디엔디라인] 도광섭 | **소품차량** [금호클래식카] 오병연 | **렉카** 강대윤 | **버스** [성산고속관광] 함성식 [유진네트워크] 장호정 | **봉고** [청호미디어] | **연출봉고** 곽귀환 김성호 | **진행봉고** 허정태 남승국 박진수 허문권 이명남 김인동 | **편집** 김인영 차영아 | **가편집** 조윤정 | **편집보조** 김다솜 김에림 | **자막** 김현민 오유니 | **음악감독** 임하영 | **작편곡** 임하영 유종현 김성율 변동욱 신민용 김완정 김지영 김달우 다니엘리 | **OST제작** 강현진 김정하 구본영 윤민아 | **Sound** [STUDIO SH] | **Sound Design** 최고은 김애정 이초희 이가영 김의선 김은광 성지영 홍예영 | **Foley** 안기성 이민섭 김현욱 | **VFX** [이든이미지웍스] | **VFX Supervisor** 하상훈 김세린 조은희 | **Compositor** 신세희 방희진 함동일 최아름 고수연 강수현 김나혜 김나랑 손혜은 곽경화 김수진 김희진 이종현 | **Motion Art** 이은경 양성빈 | **Matte Painter** 윤찬미 | **3D/FX** 이진우 RR[알투] 유신 장문수 박동진 | **VFX** [아이앤유] | **VFX Supervisor** 이현희 이성수 | **Compositor** 이슬휘 유유미 연세아 | **DI** [U5K Imageworks] | **Digital Colorist** 엄태식 | **Assistant Colorist** 강솔이 서경준 | **Technical Supervisor** 서종권, 양성원 | **DI Producer** 손민경 | **티저** [PEAK] 박상권 우정연 이학진 우선호 | **타이틀 일러스트** 차원 | **종합편집/DIT** [DH Media Works Lab] | **종합편집** 이동환 이하슬 | **데이터슈퍼바이저** 김재겸 박주현 | **DIT** 전성훈 이종찬 | **타이틀 캘리그라피** 전은선 | **대본인쇄** [슈퍼북] 김주형 권세나 | **포스터디자인** [VanD] 이용희 | **포스터사진** 강현인 | **스틸** [GARAGE LAB] 한성경 | **메이킹** [블리스 콘텐츠] 안연수 | **보조작가** 문수연 | **스토리보드** [잉크런] 유현 | **로케이션** [워킹뷰] 이슬기 정종국 | **SCR** 김부경 한소이 | **연출부** 강현 김석현 박홍탁 김영현 박기윤 박수희 권세현 | **조연출** [임과함께] 임완철 정연욱 | **원작 영화** 〈홍반장〉(글 강석범)